*Pat,*
*I followed your path.*
*Thanks for your kind*
*support and expertise.*
*Fondly,*
*Judy Comer Franklin*

# Cold Passion

by

Judy Comer Franklin

**PublishAmerica**
Baltimore

ISBN: 1-4137-1822-1
PUBLISHED BY PUBLISHAMERICA, LLLP
www.publishamerica.com
Baltimore

Printed in the United States of America

This is for Josie, with love.

# Acknowledgements

I would like to thank the following people and organizations for their invaluable support and expertise: Al Franklin for his love and belief in me and especially for the photo on the back cover; Scott and Cher Franklin for their enthusiasm as I went through this long process; Cheryl Smith Leonard for her listening skills and kind heart; Sharon L. Schultz, Tillie Ink Literary Services; Lawney Schultz; Jean McCord's Critique Group; Medical Examiner for Tacoma/Pierce County, Washington; King County Sheriff's Department, Seattle, Washington; Bureau of Land Management staff at Red Rock Canyon National Conservation Area, Las Vegas, Nevada.

# Prologue

I stood over the shallow grave of my best friend, Harvey Jordan, and his wife, Stephanie. Her body looked prim, as if she'd been posed. From this view, at the top of the mountain, Las Vegas looked like a gaudy young lady. I'd have to come up here at night to see the neon, carnival-like view of the Strip.

I hadn't told my partner, Homicide Detective Ed Daniels, that I knew the victims…

# One

"Hey! Get that news crew off the mountain," an exasperated lieutenant shouted at the uniformed police manning the yellow crime scene tape. "I thought I told you guys to keep those vultures at bay."

I couldn't stay near the gravesite any longer. If I did I'd start screaming and I couldn't do that. I listened to the lieutenant as he bullied the new recruits, and then walked over to the young policeman who looked most upset by the outburst. "The lieutenant likes to yell. Ignore the manner of how he said it, but do what he wants," I advised.

He took off his hat and wiped sweat from his glistening forehead. "Thanks, Detective Scott. I'll do my best."

New recruits to the Las Vegas Metro Police were put through a rigorous, militaristic training program. The training I'd received in Washington State so many years ago couldn't compare and sometimes I felt like I was part of the Dark Ages. If it hadn't been for Harvey Jordan back then mentoring me during my first few days out of the Academy, I wouldn't be standing here now as a homicide detective.

I slowly walked back to the gravesite and joined my partner, as he looked over the scene. "I hate to tell you this, Ed, but…"

"What, May?" he asked, clearly not paying much attention. I like Ed. He's my second favorite partner; the first being one of the victims in the grave at our feet.

"I said I have to tell you something, and now."

"Spit it out, then. Did you notice how the woman looks like she's ready to get up and go to dinner or something? She's clean, well dressed, and had a plastic tarp laid over her. The killer wanted to keep her clean, didn't he?"

"To tell you the truth, I haven't been looking all that closely because I know them. I can barely stand here without falling apart." Tears streamed down my face and along with them came my mascara and makeup. When I rubbed my face I wondered why I bothered with the mess of makeup.

"Did you just tell me you knew these people? Who are they?"

"Let's go sit in the car. I might pass out if I have to see Harvey and Stephanie like this any longer." I stumbled over a rock on the way to our unmarked police car. I hate ugly cars and this was one of the biggest, ugliest ones Ed and I had ever driven.

Ed got in and I turned the ignition so the air conditioner would come on. He, too, wiped sweat from his face with the large white handkerchief he always carried. I noticed how clean it stayed when makeup and mascara didn't rub off onto it. "I'm going to stop wearing makeup," I announced, sure this was the smartest move I would ever make.

"What're you talking about? Are you having heat stroke? Where are your sunglasses? You can't see a thing out here without them."

"I took them off when I saw Harvey and Stephanie. I couldn't stand to look at them. Call it blind self-preservation."

"Who are they?"

"Harvey Jordan and his wife, Stephanie. They married a few months ago. Remember when I went back to Tacoma for the wedding?"

"You mean this is the guy you spend so much time talking with on the phone and get all those emails from? He looks old enough to be your father. I knew Harvey was your partner in Tacoma, but I sort of figured you had something going on with him."

"He was like my father. Harvey mentored me through my first five years in the department. He taught me everything I know about police work."

"Did you know they were in Vegas?"

"Yes, I had dinner with them last Friday. Harvey was here for the police convention and Stephanie came along. We met at Caesar's

Palace, that's where they were staying. I was supposed to meet them tomorrow for lunch. They were flying back to Tacoma on Saturday."

I pulled down the visor, slid open the mirror cover and looked at my tear-swollen eyes. "I look just like I feel – like a truck ran over me and then backed up."

"Did he say anything about any trouble he might be in? Did he and his wife seem nervous?"

"No. They were perfectly normal." I closed the mirror and pushed up the visor. "We had a terrific time. In fact, I was trying my best to talk them into moving down here when Harvey retires…you know what I mean; he can't retire now," I said, stumbling over my words. Out of the corner of my eye, I saw the coroner's van drive up. The next stop for Harvey and Stephanie was going to be cold steel tables in the morgue.

"May, you know that you can't work this case."

Ed was right, but I also knew I couldn't walk away. Harvey wouldn't have done that to me if I'd been the one in the grave. I knew Ed's thoughts were accurate. I shouldn't be connected to this investigation. However, being stubborn – pigheaded, as Harvey used to call me – is a part of my nature, like the freckles that march across my nose.

I'll never understand people who say things like, "When the job isn't fun anymore I'll quit." My job has never been any fun and I've been doing it for almost twenty years. Most of my adult life has been spent in the pursuit of people who commit murder. How can this be an enjoyable occupation? No doubt, I'm good at it, but fun? I don't think so. It's the puzzle part that fascinates me and keeps me coming back. I take great pleasure in putting killers behind bars.

We drove down the mountain to the impressive sales office of the Eagle Crest housing development. It was within sight of the crime scene. When we pushed open the heavy glass door that led into the ornate lobby, a tall, blond woman in a tight, red knit dress swooped toward Ed.

"Hello, I'm Diana, salesperson extraordinaire. How can I help you?" the exotic-looking woman asked Ed, as she batted her long, false eyelashes at him. Her dress looked like spray on paint and little was left to the imagination. Ed checked her out through his sunglasses.

I went over to the silver coffee service and poured a cup, which I laced with several spoonfuls of sugar. I knew I should be with Ed as he questioned her, but I couldn't bring myself to join in their conversation. I was numb with grief and it seemed to get worse as the hours passed. I followed Ed around in a stupor, in no way helping with the investigation.

# Two

Ed drove the car back to our substation office, not far from the Fremont district. As we drove past the courthouse, people loitered around on the steps waiting for their court time. From the wedding gowns in evidence they were waiting to get married or pick up their licenses. Some of the brides looked a bit shopworn to me and I wondered how many times they'd stood on these steps in the same bedraggled dresses.

Ed pulled into the parking lot and quickly turned the car into our slot.

"You need to tell Lieutenant Frank about knowing the victims," he said as we got out of the car.

I agreed and followed him into the office. We stayed about an hour and most of the time I was in a daze. However, I didn't talk to the lieutenant. I knew what he'd say and I wasn't ready to hear it.

After he'd started files on the murders, Ed and I headed back out to the car, on our way to the morgue. I looked up at him and said, "I know you're right about me walking away, but I can't, at least not now."

"May, please, just this one time in your long hard-headed life, listen to me. I'm going to have to ask you questions about the time you spent with the victims. How do you think I feel about that? You're my partner, but I'll have to treat you just like I treat everyone else I interview. There's nothing good about this situation and you're making it worse."

"I'll stay just until we've talked to Dr. Williams, then I'll go see

Lieutenant Frank."

"I know this is terrible for you. Are you sure you want to go to the morgue?"

"I have to. I couldn't live with myself if I didn't."

"I wouldn't be doing any of this, but that's me. After talking with Dr. Williams, you'll tell the lieutenant. Right?"

"Right."

Usually we take back streets but Ed, maybe to put off the inevitable, took the slower route through the heart of Las Vegas, commonly called "The Strip". He knew I didn't want to see Harvey and Stephanie lying on those cold steel tables.

No matter how many times I've been on this street, it still fascinates me. It's easy to understand why tourists from all over the world come here. It was a little early in the day for the usual throngs of people who crowd the Strip's wide sidewalks. Activity goes on twenty-four hours a day, but when the sun starts to go down, this street comes throbbing to noisy life. Giant billboards run endless advertisements for club shows. Taxis, buses, moving sidewalks, monorails, and rental cars ferry people to and from the attractions that line the Strip. Multi-colored, razzle-dazzle neon lights glow constantly, day and night.

After we'd turned right off the Strip and onto the wide street that led to the morgue, Las Vegas looked like any southwest city. I've often wondered how many of the tourists, who spent their time and money on the Strip, venture away from it to see how the residents lived. I think they'd be surprised at the similarity to their towns and neighborhoods. Of course, since I arrived eight years ago the city had more than doubled in size and population.

"I thought since you didn't get lunch we'd stop by your favorite coffee shop. Are you hungry?" Ed asked.

"I couldn't eat a thing, but I'll be glad to sit with you while you get something."

"I grabbed a quick bite back at the station."

"I'll eat later. I can't now."

"Are you still sure you want to see them?"

"No, I don't want to do this, but I have to. I have to prove to myself that they're dead, that it wasn't some horrible nightmare. Am I asleep and when I wake up it'll all be gone?"

"I'm afraid, May, this is about as real as it gets."

As much as I tried to avoid reality it was now in front of me. The morgue is located in a new building, and there is nothing on the outside to indicate what goes on inside. Ed parked the car and we walked into the building and toward a bank of elevators. He entered a code on the numeric keypad, the doors slid silently open and we got on. When it stopped and the doors re-opened, I saw the wide double swinging doors of the morgue. I put one foot in front of the other, but I did not want to go into that room. I heard a faint noise and knew Ed was talking to me as he punched in another number code, but it was incoherent to me. He held open one of the heavy doors and I saw Dr. Williams, the Medical Examiner. Beyond his large bulk, two sheet-covered forms lay on the steel tables. The tiled room was very clean and cold. There was a slight antiseptic, sweet smell from the wall-mounted deodorizer. I felt as though I'd turned to stone.

I went back in time, to the day when I'd been in a similar situation in Montana. I'd been at a junior high football game and I was so excited because we were wearing our new cheerleader outfits when the police car, with its flashing lights, pulled near the packed stands. Somehow I knew that they were there for me. The game stopped as two uniformed officers walked onto the field. They asked that I follow them back to their car. When I was in the backseat, they told me about my parents. They'd been on the way to the game and had been killed in a head-on collision caused by a drunken driver. That's why I rarely drink; I've seen what it can do to the human body. The man who killed them got off with some community service work. Later, he drank himself to death. So alcohol kills in all sorts of ways.

That day was far in the past, but as I looked at Harvey and then Stephanie, I felt as though my parents had died all over again. Black spots swam in front of my eyes as I crumpled slowly to the floor. Arms lifted me up and carried me out of the cold room. I felt like I had when I'd come close to drowning. I knew what was going on but I couldn't control it and I was so very cold.

When I came to, I was lying on a couch in Dr. Williams' office. I had sat on this couch many times before. Lying on it was a new experience and one I didn't like. He told me to lay back and keep still, that I might be in shock. I pushed his hands away and pulled myself up to a sitting position.

"Here, drink this water," Dr. Williams said.

I usually hate drinking water, but it tasted good. I asked for more, drinking it greedily. My brain was starting to unclog and I teetered to my feet. "Thank you both. I had no idea I was going to react that way."

"I see all sorts of reactions in here. Yours was fairly easy to fix," he said. "Ed tells me you knew the victims."

"Yes. I worked with Harvey for almost twelve years in Tacoma. I was 'best man' at their wedding a few months ago."

"You shouldn't be working this case," Dr. Williams said. "You work too hard and this isn't good for you. Listen to me because you know it's the truth."

"I know in my head you're both right, but my heart tells me something different. I promised Ed that I'd back away after we'd talked with you."

Ed, who'd been silent, spoke up. "So, Doc, what can you tell us? I know they were both shot in the head at close range. Have you found anything else that can help us?"

I mouthed a silent "thank you" to Ed and turned my attention back to Dr. Williams.

"They were killed instantly by one shot each to the head, as you said, at close range. There was no sign of struggle and, unless the lab tests prove me wrong, nothing indicates they were drugged. By the condition of the bodies, they've been dead about forty-eight hours, which places the time of death at sometime Tuesday evening. The bodies arrived about thirty minutes ago. Obviously, I haven't had time to do a full autopsy. I can tell you more when that's been completed."

"The convention Harvey was attending started on Sunday and ends this Friday. That means we need to start interviewing people immediately," I said.

"Did you talk with Harvey and Stephanie during the week?" Ed asked. "You and Harvey are always on the phone, so he must have called."

"He did, but to tell the truth, it was messages on both ends. We really didn't talk in person; we just kept leaving all these messages."

"I'll need your phone recordings. A team is already at Caesar's Palace. I suggest you and I join them," Ed commented.

I nodded my head in agreement. I turned to Dr. Williams and gave him a quick hug. "Thanks for helping me."

"I'm sorry about your loss and I'll do all I can to help the detectives get this case solved quickly. You take some time off. And thanks for the hug. It's rare that my patients hug me."

# Three

Traffic on the Strip was in gridlock. "Did I ever tell you that one of the main reasons I left the Puget Sound area was the traffic? I couldn't deal with it. So, now, here I am in Las Vegas sitting in backed-up traffic."

"Yeah, you've told me that sad tale about a thousand times. I'll get us out of this mess," he said, with a gleam in his eye. Actually, I couldn't see his eyes because of his sunglasses, but I knew there was a gleam in there somewhere.

We roared through side streets and back alleys and broke several laws along the way to Caesar's Palace, always my favorite hotel on the Strip.

"You promised you'd talk to the lieutenant."

"I will. Every word that you and Dr. Williams said to me is true. What do you think he meant by saying his patients hugged him? Do they crawl out from under those sheets and hug him?"

"I saw you turn a shade paler. He was trying to take your mind off."

The car took up two spaces in the parking lot reserved for official vehicles, due to Ed's tire-screaming job of parking. I shook my head but didn't say anything. I figured I'd done enough to Ed for one day.

"Did you go to their room?" he asked.

"No. We had dinner in the Forum restaurant and then walked around the casino. They were going to gamble. That's where I last saw them alive." Tears ran down my cheeks and I brushed them away before Ed could see them.

If this was a recession I couldn't tell it. It looked like a normal day in Las Vegas. The cobble stoned streets and realistic skies of the Forum Shops were mobbed with tourists.

When we reached the bank of elevators that took guests to their rooms, we had to show our badges to get through the crowd that was clustered in front of the doors.

Harvey, who'd been frugal, had picked an expensive suite of rooms. Maybe a delayed honeymoon, I thought, but remembered they'd gone to Hawaii soon after their wedding. The suite and part of the hall was ringed with bright yellow crime scene tape.

"Do you think they were killed at the mountain site or somewhere else?" I asked Ed.

"They were killed on the mountain. It resembled a gangland hit – clean, cold, and passionless. If it was twenty years ago, I'd be looking through mob files."

"Who talked to the boys who found the bodies?"

"I did while you were off in your own world."

He told me that two teenage boys had accidentally found the bodies hidden under a few feet of dirt. When they rode their bikes to the top of the mountain and stopped to look at the view, their tires had sunk into the freshly dug graves. It was in the section of a construction site that wasn't set for development until the current crop of homes had sold.

It dawned on me that I'd suggested Harvey and Stephanie drive up there and go through the model homes. I'd gone through several of them myself and was impressed with the place. "Oh no!"

"Oh no what?" Ed asked.

"I was trying to get them to move down here. I can't believe it's where they died."

Ed and I went into the suite and it teemed with forensic activity. I was glad to see my friend Janet. We'd met soon after I came to Las Vegas and immediately clicked. Her high cheek-boned African-American face glowed with health and intelligence.

"May, I know you won't be coming over this afternoon like we'd planned. I'm so sorry to hear that you knew the victims. Frankie will be disappointed but he'll understand."

Frankie, her teenage son, called me "Mom Number Two" and had done that since we'd met eight years ago. I'd been his favorite babysitter, though he hated the term. In his eyes, I was his surrogate mother and I loved him as if he were my son. When he was younger, Janet and I took him to watch the pirate ship and the English frigate battle it out in front of the Treasure Island Hotel. We must have seen the pirate show fifty times and I enjoyed it almost as much as Frankie did. Now, he was almost grown. It was a good thing that Janet and I could console each other when he left for college in a year.

"Give him my love. Have you found anything that can get us headed in a direction?" I asked.

"It's too soon. Until we can get into the lab and examine what we've got, I won't be able to tell you anything. But you'll be the first person I'll call."

"Call me," Ed requested. "May's not going to work this case." Ed paused a moment, then asked, "By the way, how did you know she knew the victims?"

"The other officers at the scene saw how May reacted and figured she knew them."

Ed and Janet looked at me and I knew what they were thinking. By now, Lieutenant Frank had heard about this.

"I'll get off the case just as soon as Ed and I do some work here. We'll check with the front desk and track down the people registered on this floor. Also, we need to get started on the convention attendees. We may have to stop their departures."

"I'll get the attendees' names and you check out this floor, May. You and I both realize that the lieutenant knows about this already."

Ed had a thing about guilt. He could make me feel it faster than my cat; both of them were masters at making me twist in the wind.

"I'll talk to him as soon as I finish interviews on this floor."

We took the elevator down to the first floor and headed for the registration lobby, which is one of the most spectacular in the city – opulent golden colors, beautifully upholstered silk chairs and couches, crystal and marble. Everything glistened and gleamed.

"We need to speak with the manager, please," I said to the man at the desk, as we showed him our badges.

"I'm sorry. She's not available at this time. Could I be of assistance?" Mel was in his mid-thirties, dressed impeccably and had multiple rings on his fingers. I knew his name was Mel and that he was a Customer Assistant because it said so on his nametag.

"We're investigating a double homicide and need names of all the people who stayed on the 35th floor over the last seven days." We showed him our badges.

"I'm sorry, we don't give out that sort of information. Our guests are very private individuals and we honor that," Mel said, certain that he was giving the correct response.

"You haven't worked long in this job, have you, Mel? We need the information quickly. Thank you for your cooperation."

"Uh, let me just check one little thing. I'll be right back." He scurried into the offices behind the front desk.

He came back, another man in tow and I had to go through the explanation again. I glanced back. Ed watched a beautiful cocktail waitress as she walked past in her revealing Roman costume.

Jeff said exactly what I wanted to hear. "We'll have that for you in just a minute. Mel, go get a printout of anything the detectives want. Caesar's Palace always supports our Las Vegas Metro Police."

"Did the hotel have many attendees staying here for the Police Convention? I know the Bellagio hosted it this year," Ed asked. The leggy waitress looked at Ed with interest.

"We did have quite a few of the police officers staying with us. Would you like that list as well?" Mel now understood how things worked.

"Thank you," Ed said, finally noticing Mel.

After we had our respective lists, he went his way and I went mine. Some of the conventioneers had been on the same floor as Harvey and Stephanie, so I decided to start with them.

When I returned to the 35th floor, the pain of Harvey's death washed over me and stopped me in my tracks. I took a few moments to gather my composure. I walked down the long corridor to a window and looked out. The sun was shining and I enjoyed feeling the warmth on my skin. I stayed there a few minutes and then walked back to the rooms, ready to begin the investigation.

# Four

I started with the room closest to Harvey and Stephanie's. When I knocked, I didn't expect an answer. I figured the guest, a Mrs. Josephine Bride, would be elsewhere in the hotel or on the Strip. I was wrong on all counts.

"Who is it?" called a small voice through the big door.

"Las Vegas Metro Police, Detective May Scott. Please open the door."

I heard the sound of the chain being removed from the door and a petite, gray haired woman looked warily into the hall. "Can I see your badge, Officer?" she asked.

I held my badge close to the door so she could see it. "Could I come in, Mrs. Bride? I have a few questions concerning the couple who were staying in the room next to you."

She opened the door and looked me up and down. "You don't look like a police officer," she announced.

"I look too small to be able to do this job, don't I?"

"I'm petite myself, so I know what that's like. You're too pretty to be a police officer. Is your hair really that color or do you dye it red?" she asked.

"It used to be reddish blond, but now that I'm turning gray, I color it."

"Well, it looks attractive on you so I guess you can come in. You remind me of my niece. She won some sort of beauty title, except she's a lot taller than you. I don't have many visitors, except for the housekeeping staff who come through each day."

Seeing that I didn't understand her comment she explained. "I rent this room a month at a time. They keep a few rooms aside, and during the off-season, they rent them out. I've stayed in all the hotels in Las Vegas at one time or the other, but this is what I consider home," she said.

"So you don't stray too far from your room?" I queried.

"No, not too often. I do go down for my evening meal, but other than that, I like it here. It has certainly been exciting for the past few hours. What happened next door?"

"We're trying to find out information about the couple who stayed there. Did you hear or see anything unusual over the last few days?"

"No. I did meet them on the elevator, though. They were such a nice couple. I do hope nothing has happened to them."

"When did you ride in the elevator with them?"

"Let's see. It must have been Monday, because on Monday they have my favorite meal, roast beef, in the dining room. I have a set menu, because of the type of guest I am, you see," she told me in way of explanation.

"Were they coming to their room or going out?"

"They were going out. I remember the woman; I believe her name was Stephanie, just like my niece. She won the beauty title. Remember I told you about her? That's how I recall her name, don't you know. Anyway, she was all dressed up. They looked so happy."

"Did you hear them when they came back to the room?

"No, but I try to mind my own business. They were very quiet, too. I noticed that right away with them. Sometimes it's very noisy, especially if it's a real young couple. Did you say something happened to them?"

"I said that right now we're investigating and I'm not at liberty to discuss it. Here's my card. Please call me if you remember anything else. Thanks for seeing me." I smiled as I opened the door to leave her room.

"Oh, it was a pleasant visit. Stop by anytime. And I really like your red hair," she said. "I just hope that nice couple hasn't gotten into any trouble. What did you say was the name of the hair color you use?"

"Persimmon Surprise."

I closed the door and wondered if I'd be in her situation in a few years. It appeared to be a very lonely life, but then maybe it wasn't. I've learned that nothing is ever as black or white as it seems.

The next door I knocked on was the room of another woman, Anne Lambert. For some reason, the name sounded familiar to me, but I couldn't place it. I knocked several times, but she either wasn't in, or was ignoring me. I scribbled a note for her to call me and stuck it in the door trim.

The next few doors got the same treatment. I wasn't surprised that most of the rooms were empty, their occupants enjoying all that Las Vegas had to offer.

I took my cell phone out of my pocket and called Ed. "It's me. I'm about to leave the hotel and go back up the mountain. Pick up or call me back now," I requested, knowing he'd have more rooms to visit since he was at the Bellagio, the primary hotel for the convention. My cell phone beeped and I unsnapped it to answer.

"Ed?"

"How did you get through so quick? I'm still up to my armpits in rooms. Did you have any luck?"

"Not much. Spoke to one older lady who was in, but at this point she hasn't provided much information. She did ride down in the elevator with them on Monday evening. Stephanie looked very dressed up, which matches with what we saw this morning. No one else was home, so I left my card all over the place, mostly stuck in doors. I want to go back up the mountain. Do you want to go with me or do you want me to help you out over there?" I asked.

"Wait for me, May. Don't go running off on your own. Come over here and help me, then we can both go back."

As usual, Ed was right. And as usual, I was going to ignore what he said. "I think I'll go on up. I'll take the car and you can catch a ride back to the station with one of the crime lab guys. Or maybe that cocktail waitress can give you a ride. See you." I quickly snapped my phone shut because I didn't want to hear him yell.

I went back down to the parking garage and drove the unmarked car onto the Strip. I must admit I liked the low rumble of the engine. It reminded me of a big purring cat. If I didn't stop myself, I might start to like this monstrosity of a car.

This wasn't a drive I wanted to make but I needed to revisit the place where Harvey and Stephanie died. I knew Ed should be with me, but somehow this was one trip I needed to make by myself. I turned left onto the Strip. As I passed the Mirage Hotel the volcano erupted in a spectacular display of fire, smoke, and water much to the delight of the tourists who crowded the wide walkways.

Billboards announcing the presence of the new housing development, Eagle Crest, seemed to spring up from the desert floor. I followed them to the community's four-lane entry point. The landscapers had turned the brown desert into a beautiful palm-littered oasis. On the right, a lush golf course sparkled with fountains, waterfalls, and pools. It looked more like a water park than a golf course. By the time I entered the parking lot, I felt guiltier than usual about leaving Ed behind so I called him.

"Ed, please call me. I'm sorry."

I sat in the car holding my cell phone. It didn't ring.

"I've done it now. And I have to stop talking to myself."

I'm sure the people milling around the parking lot, if they heard me, thought I was nuts. I climbed out of the car, locked it, and walked toward the huge entrance doors of the sales office.

I opened the heavy door and walked over to the glass windows that overlooked the golf course, and below, Las Vegas.

"Did you sign our guest register?" cooed a strange voice.

"No, I'm afraid I just wandered over here. I was overcome by the view," I replied to Diana, which was on her nametag. It seemed everybody in this town wore a nametag. I remembered that Ed had interviewed her earlier.

Diana tinkled a merry little laugh and asked that I follow her swaying backside to the lobby. "It's just to keep track of our visitors," she said in a breathy Marilyn Monroe imitation.

I guess this is the sort of job a Las Vegas showgirl gets when she's too old for the shows. Although I had to admit, Diana looked terrific, if a little plastic. Everything was perfectly in place.

"Diana is such a pretty name," I said, trying to butter her up.

"Yes, I changed my name to Diana after the Princess died in that car crash in Paris," she said, batting her long eyelashes at me.

I stared at her, speechless. I came to my senses, pulled out my badge and asked to look at the sign-in sheets.

"Why?" she asked, her voice changing to a whole other octave.

"As you know, there were two bodies found at the top of the mountain, within the boundaries of this housing project. We need to check dates and times of visitors."

"I can't give out that sort of information. It's private and you don't have a warrant," she spat out. "Anyway, a whole bunch of cops have already been through here, including you."

I should give her Mel's name and number. They might make a match, except she was so much taller that he was. "The faster we get these murders solved, the sooner we'll be out of your hair," I explained. "We can do this my way, which will be quick or your way, which means you and I could be here all night." I was trying to make her life easier.

"Oh, all right. I have a date tonight so I won't spend the night with you." She turned back to a cabinet and produced a clipboard.

I quickly scanned the names and saw that Harvey and Stephanie had signed in last Sunday afternoon. I was about to give it back to Diana when my eye caught another name I recognized, Anne Lambert.

"Do you remember this couple, or this woman?" I asked a clearly peeved Diana.

"I've already told those policemen earlier today that I don't recall anything about any of this. Now, are we through?"

"Just one more thing. Don't you have people fill out a sheet with information on where they live and work?"

"I send those over to corporate headquarters in Phoenix. We don't keep them here."

26

I thought that was strange, but decided not to grill her about it. I'd get back to Diana later.

"Oh, and by the way, are these roads open to the public at night? I noticed you have a large entry gate off the main road. Is it a key or password system to get up here?"

"Only in the areas where the houses are occupied. Until all the lots have been sold, it's open."

"So I can come up here at night?" I quizzed.

"Yes, you can," Diana responded, clearly wanting me out the door.

I walked out to the car, unlocked it, and slid behind the wheel. My phone beeped and I pulled it out of my purse and answered, "Ed?"

"Yes, and who is this? Not my partner. You know, the one who left me stranded in the middle of Las Vegas?"

"I apologize. Are you still stranded? I can come pick you up. I'll be there in twenty minutes, tops."

"Never mind. Janet gave me a ride back downtown. When are you arriving, by the way? And where are you?"

I could tell this conversation was going downhill fast. "I'm at the housing development. I was just going up to the murder scene."

"No, don't do that. Come back here. I have some things we need to discuss. And it's about a certain lieutenant who found out one of his detectives is working on a case and she knew both victims, and didn't tell him. Get your skinny butt back here, now, and explain this to the boss."

"I'm on my way." I put my head down on the steering wheel and thought about crying but I was too tired.

I was within view of the gravesite from the parking lot. I started the car and drove slowly out of the lot, turning right onto the paved highway. I drove up the hill, passed the murder site, and then turned the car around at the end of the pavement. Houses wouldn't be built here until the ones below had been sold.

I parked the car on the side of the road, got out, and walked toward the crime scene tape. I pulled a section of it up and crouched underneath it to get to the other side. The sandy soil was dry and when I kicked at it dust swirled around. I wondered if Stephanie's body had been covered by the plastic tarp to keep her clean, as Ed had mentioned. Harvey didn't have a covering over his body. In the killer's mind, that must mean something. Maybe Stephanie hadn't been the main target and the killer wanted to "protect" her, in some crazy way.

Because Harvey had been a homicide detective for so long, my gut told me he was the one the killer wanted. Perhaps Stephanie had been covered as a sort of, "I'm sorry to do this to you," gesture. Murders rarely made sense, except in the disturbed mind of the killer.

It was quiet on top of the mountain. Cars didn't come up this far. Building hadn't started for this section, so the large machines that tore the earth apart were silent, sitting off to the side. It was a shame they couldn't talk, because they'd witnessed the murders.

The wind blew constantly and I put my hand over my eyes to shade them as I looked in all directions around the site. To the left, the Strip glittered like fool's gold. Each hotel built seemed to be taller and gaudier, feeding the tourist frenzy for something newer, bigger, better. Construction ringed the city, and with so many housing developments, malls, and roads being built, city maps couldn't keep up with the changes. Over a million and a half permanent residents lived in the valley. Tourists on a monthly basis pushed the number to over two million. Someone, in this place I loved to call home, had killed Harvey and Stephanie and I had no idea why.

# Five

My small, white stucco rambler with the red tiled roof is located in one of the older areas of Las Vegas. Purple bougainvillea has grown up over the side of the house and a portion of the roof. When it's in bloom, it's spectacular.

I bought the house soon after I got my job with the Las Vegas Metro Police. It's not fancy but it'd been lovingly taken care of by the couple who'd built it in the fifty's. They'd moved back East to be nearer to their grandchildren. I can see the Stratosphere from my yard if I twist my neck into a yoga pose. There's grass and large trees in my backyard, which most people don't expect.

A garage used to be attached to the house but the couple had converted it into a lanai; what we called a porch back in Montana and a covered deck in Washington. Because the weather in Nevada is cooperative I grow tomatoes, peppers and flowers year round. In the early morning and late afternoon, even if the day has been blistering hot, I sit outside and enjoy the silky-warm feel of the air. Unfortunately I hear street noise, since I'm not far off the Strip.

I'd sold my house in Tacoma's North End and planned to use the money to pay off credit card bills. If there was any money left, I wanted to remodel my kitchen, which still had fifty's-era appliances. I hadn't wanted to sell the house in Tacoma because it was my last connection to the Northwest; Harvey had talked me into it. And since he was so good with finances I'd listened.

Moving to Nevada had been the right decision, even if it had been made for emotional reasons. I wanted to get away from Dan, my ex-husband, his wife Connie, who had been his administrative assistant, and their twin baby girls. Dan and I were married only a few months when he left me for Connie, his "soul mate."

Harvey and his first wife Vicky had consoled me through the worst of it. Later I got to console Harvey when his beloved Vicky had died of ovarian cancer. That's when he and I had developed the close bond that still existed, even though he was now dead.

I pulled the car into the driveway, got out, walked to the front door and unlocked it. My cat Whiskers was waiting on the windowsill and gave me "the look" when I entered the house. I've never figured out how an animal that weighs less than ten pounds can cause me such guilt. I put my purse down and scooped her up. She purred loudly in my ear as I carried her into the kitchen then put her on the floor. She wound in and out of my legs while I scrambled around and found her favorite tuna. People tuna, not that disgusting version for cats. By the time I had it in her dish, which I'd quickly cleaned, she'd forgiven me. I got her comb off the windowsill and gently raked it through her long, black-and-white fur. She enjoyed being combed; I tried to do it at least once a day.

I half-heartedly listened to my messages, knowing that Harvey's voice was going to be on several of them. I had to remember to give Ed my password so he could access my messages.

I scratched Whiskers under the chin and she purred contentedly. I decided to take a quick shower and change clothes. I can get into and out of the shower in record time. I was back in the car in less than twenty minutes. Whiskers hopped up onto the windowsill to watch me go.

Since I live so close to work, I got to the office in less than ten minutes. After parking, I slowly made my way to the station door. As I pondered whether I could fake an emergency dental procedure to get away from Lieutenant Frank, the doors slid open. I walked to my desk, put my purse in a side drawer, and headed for his office. I saw his shiny, bald head bent over paperwork, as it usually was. He was one of those types who liked being in his office doing paperwork.

That sort of stuff drove me wild. I did all I could to push it off on Ed. Before Ed, Harvey had done it for me. Of course, that meant I did things for them that they hated doing. As it turned out, both of them disliked public speaking. I enjoy doing that, especially when it involves elementary school-age kids. It was a fair system, a "you scratch my back and I'll scratch yours" arrangement.

I tapped on the open door to get his attention.

"May, I've been expecting you. Come in and close the door, please." He pointed at a chair across from his desk.

I thought, *Heaven help me,* as I closed the door and sat down across from his large desk.

"I've assigned Brenda Mitchell to work with Ed." Brenda always said the right thing and followed every rule; most people liked her. I thought she was as plastic as Diana, the salesperson at Eagle's Crest. But then, as Ed told me, I was jealous of her because she was young and cute. I didn't buy that. Still, hearing that Brenda was going to be working on Harvey and Stephanie's murder set my teeth on edge.

"Couldn't I work background issues on this case, Lieutenant? I knew both of them; especially Harvey. Ed and Brenda don't know anything about them."

He looked at me over the top of his glasses and shook his head, "No. What you can do, though, is take some time off. You've got vacation leave to burn and now is the time to use it. Go home, see some shows, tan at the Mandalay Bay Hotel beach; just don't come back here for at least two weeks. You're a good, instinctive detective, but you have no regard for procedure. You and I've had this conversation before, usually around evaluation time. That you've lasted this long in police work amazes me. Maybe because you've helped solve some high profile murders using your, shall we say, unorthodox methods. This time, though, you've got to do it by the book and get out of the way of the investigation. Your instincts will be way off because of your emotional involvement. I don't want to see you here, May. Do you understand what I'm telling you?"

I recognized by his tone that he wouldn't change his mind, but I had to try. "I'm just supposed to walk meekly away from the murder investigation of my best friend? Would you do that?"

"Yes, I would. I just explained that to you. No, I'm not going to let you work on this case. I'm sorry for your loss, May. Please leave the door open on your way out." He burrowed back into his pile of papers. I understood what he'd said but knew I wasn't going to follow orders. Yes, I would be out of the office; but no, I wasn't going to let Harvey and Stephanie's murderer be caught by anyone except me.

I walked into the open office area and ran right into Ernie, a man I'd had a serious crush on when I first arrived in Las Vegas. He used to work in the hotel shows as a dancer. I always suspected he became a motorcycle cop because he knew how great he looked in his tight uniform and tall black boots. You couldn't dispute the guy was gorgeous and most of the time he was nice.

"I heard about your trouble, May. I stopped by to see if you needed any help. You know I'm there for you, kid." He brushed back a lock of his golden hair and I observed once more that he looked like a movie star. Janet had told me from day one that he was trouble. Over the years, she'd listened to my sad tales of woe about Ernie. She called him a "serial womanizer". No wonder Ed and Harvey had tried so hard to set me up with someone they approved of, and that most definitely wasn't "Mr. Golden Boy."

"Thanks, I'll let you know if there's anything I need."

"You know Uncle Ernie is your best friend, don't you?" he asked, with that dimpled, killer smile.

"My best friend is lying in the morgue right now. Excuse me, I've got to go. Thanks for the offer."

"If you need a little extra friendship give me a call, if you get my drift."

As he slid away, like the snake he sometimes was, I couldn't believe I'd let myself get so obsessed with him.

On my way out the door, I noticed that my phone light was blinking. I sat down in my desk chair and swiveled around to check it. The first message was from a lawyer whose name I didn't catch, so I replayed it. "This is for May Scott. Please call me, Rick Purdue, at this number. I'm a partner in Purdue, Wesson, and Jeffreys Law

Firm. I need to speak to you about a private legal matter."

The number was in Las Vegas, so I called it right away. An official sounding woman connected me to his voice mail. "This is May Scott returning your call. You can also reach me at my cell number," which I provided.

I listened to the other messages, returned calls, and left the information that I was out of the office on my voice mail. I referred calls to Ed, knowing he would diligently call back each and every one.

Having completed that chore, I was about to start cleaning out my desk drawers when Lieutenant Frank stepped out of his office and saw me. He shook his head, clearly exasperated with me, and pointed to the exit doorway.

I left the police car in the lot and drove my car home. As I pulled into the drive, I saw Whiskers watching me from the windowsill. *At least somebody was left to love me*, I thought. Fat, hot tears streamed down my face and I put my head on the steering wheel. This had been one of the worst days of my life and it was only four p.m.

# Six

I stayed home for a few hours and actually managed to take a catnap. I felt better when I woke up and decided that I should drive back up the mountain, no matter what Ed said. Before I left, however, I called him and left a message. I scratched Whiskers under the chin and pulled on her long, white whiskers, which is how she got her name. When she'd been a kitten, her whiskers were longer than she was. I paid a dollar for her, in the garden shop where I first saw her, and it was the best investment I'd ever made.

I started the car and drove toward the development. It was a beautiful night. The air was pleasant and the sky was filled with stars. I passed attractive, new subdivisions, malls, and hospitals. It looked like any nice town in America, with palm trees and desert. As I drove away from the Strip, it wasn't long before I was back in the desert. The Strip was only minutes away and a world apart.

The entrance to Eagle Crest was well lighted, as I'd expected. I drove onto the newly paved road to the model home area. There was something about Diana that bothered me, so I decided to snoop. I pulled onto a side road, stopped the car and got out. The view was incredible. Las Vegas and the entire valley were lit up beyond belief. The laser light from the Luxor Hotel beamed straight up from the pyramid's tip far into the night sky. It was quiet, peaceful, and beautiful; then I heard a car engine.

I turned my head to the right but didn't see anything. To the left a dark-colored car, with no lights on, rolled slowly around the corner. I stepped back into the bushes and crouched down. As it passed by I saw that the driver had on a dark, hooded top. I couldn't tell if it was a man or woman. I picked out most of the numbers from the license plate and the make of the car as it continued to creep its way down the road. At the stop sign, the driver turned down the hill, turned on the lights, picked up speed, and was quickly gone.

I stepped out of my hiding place and watched, as the taillights got smaller. I wondered what he'd been looking for. Maybe he'd left something at the murder scene or just wanted to return to the site. On the other hand, it could mean nothing.

I decided to try and discover what Diana was up to, which was why I'd come up here in the first place. I walked around the corner of the building and saw that a car was still parked outside the entrance to the model home area. A light shone through the large doors. I caught a glimpse of Diana as she turned off the light and closed the building I walked to the back where my small, nondescript car sat, turned on the engine, kept the lights off, and waited for her to drive past. I called Ed and left the information on his voice mail about the other car's number and make.

Diana drove by and didn't notice me. After she'd gone down the hill, I turned on my lights and followed her. She drove slowly, which surprised me. It was hard for me to slow down my speed to stay far enough back that she didn't see me. She drove out of the city, toward Red Rock Canyon, and turned left into the small town of Blue Diamond. It consisted of a few streets, houses, a store, church, post office, and school. You could walk around the place in about five minutes.

I pulled off to the side of the road and watched the car's taillights. I followed slowly and found where she'd parked, in front of the garage door of a run down house. Most of the houses in Blue Diamond were very attractive, but this wasn't one of them. It was hard to imagine that not-a-hair-out-of-place Diana lived in this fixer-upper.

I watched from down the street as the garage door slid upward, she got out of the car and walked into the house. It was easy to see why she didn't pull the car into the garage. It was packed with boxes and other odds and ends. It looked like a bunch of junk from where I sat, but I guess it must have been treasures to her. She lowered the door and I rolled the car forward to see if I could catch other glimpses of her through the windows. She turned on lights as she went, and then came to the very windows I was watching and pulled the drapes. I pulled forward again, turned the car around, so I was headed in the out direction. In this town, all streets were dead ends or circles and she was on a dead end.

Blue Diamond ended almost as soon as it started and didn't march up the mountains that were directly behind it. I knew that people who lived in Blue Diamond protected their privacy. This was a small, close-knit community whose citizens did not like or tolerate outsiders. It was an on-going battle for the residents of Blue Diamond to keep developers away from the area.

A police officer that I'd worked with on several cases lived here and referred to it as "heaven on earth." I'd been to a party at his house once and when I drove up, there were four wild horses eating grass in his front yard. They weren't afraid of people and were used to kind treatment.

"I usually have burros in my yard," he'd commented. "So it's nice to have the horses visit."

The lights in Diana's house clicked off and the house went dark. I heard the rumble of her ancient garage door as it creaked upward. My eyebrows rose as I watched a tall, slender man with a crew cut walk toward Diana's car and get in. He turned on the ignition and the car rolled slowly into the street. I let him wind down the hill until he got to the main road. Only then did I start my car and follow him.

I kept at a discreet distance, which was fairly simple since the man was such a deliberate, slow driver, just like Diana. It's not smart following possible murder suspects around in the dark and I knew Ed would be livid when he heard about this.

By this time we'd driven into West Las Vegas and he pulled into a club parking lot. I drove past and watched as he got out of the car and walked toward the entrance to the Choices Club. I'd never heard of it, but that didn't mean much. I pulled into a drugstore parking lot, turned around, and drove back to the club. I mulled over the wisdom of going into this situation by myself, and then thought, *well, why not.* I made a fast call to Ed and left a message telling him where I was.

I got out of the car, locked it, and headed toward the club entrance. I had no idea what type of club it was, but I hoped it was crowded. If the parking lot was any indication, it was. There wasn't a cover charge and there were wall-to-wall bodies. This was all very good.

What wasn't so good was that, as far as I could tell, all of the bodies belonged to men and I couldn't easily blend in. Luckily, the man I'd followed was so busy dirty dancing that he wasn't paying any attention, unlike about a hundred others, who had their eyes glued on me. I slunk back against the wall and found a seat at a small table near the men's room. There wasn't a women's room, which didn't surprise me.

A waiter came over and asked what I wanted to drink. I ordered a diet soda and asked if he knew the name of the really cute guy who was dancing on top of the table. "That's Dickie Patty. He's so hot," he said, and rolled his eyes. I nodded in agreement and watched as Dickie writhed to the throbbing, intense music. The man could certainly move, in a vulgar sort of way. It wasn't making me tingle anywhere, but for the hundred or so men in here, Dickie was a star.

I sat there long enough to get the full effect of Dickie then I stayed as close to the wall as possible on my way to the exit. The night air felt wonderful after the steam bath atmosphere of the club. All those hot bodies were too much for me. I got back in the car and pulled out my phone. I just had to share this little tidbit with Ed, that is, if he was still speaking to me. He answered on the first ring, which I took as a positive sign.

"Ed, you aren't going to believe this one."

Clearly exasperated, he asked, "Where are you this time?"

"I'm at the Choices Club in West Las Vegas. You'll never guess about Diana."

"Who's Diana?"

"Diana is the salesperson at Eagle Crest. Remember? Tall, blond, built?"

"I remember the tall blond."

"You couldn't get your eyes off her boobs or backside."

"Oh, yeah, she was built."

"Uh, huh, and her other name is Dickie Patty, lives in Blue Diamond, and has a crew cut."

"Are you telling me she's a he?"

"Yep. I just watched him make a roomful of guys pant. Dickie is quite the entertainer."

"That doesn't mean he's not the killer. In fact, we had her, I mean him, on our list to re-question tomorrow."

"You and Brenda? How's she working out, by the way? Makes you miss me, doesn't it? Come on, tell the truth."

"Yes, I sort of miss you. But she follows rules, and it's nice knowing I can count on her not to leave me hanging."

This conversation wasn't going in a direction I liked. "I don't do things on purpose; I do them because I get so caught up in the moment. Anyway, I'm not getting a warm fuzzy that Dickie's the killer. He's got too much going on, what with all his costume changes. Did you have a chance to track down the plates on that car I saw up at Eagle Crest?"

"Not yet; I did call it in, though. Did you go back up to the crime scene?"

"I did earlier today but not this evening. I decided to follow Diana, who morphed into Dickie. I still think something isn't quite right with that development, but I'll worry about that later. Have you run across anything that might be worth looking into?" I asked, relieved to be talking to my partner.

"I can't say that we have. We'll be going back to the convention hotel tomorrow and talk to that older lady you spoke with. What was her name?"

"Mrs. Josephine Bride. There was another name on the hotel list that I also saw on the model homes list. Anne Lambert. For some reason, that name sounds familiar to me."

"I haven't talked to her, but I recall seeing her signature on the sign-in sheet. Who is she?"

"I don't know, other than she was on the same floor as Harvey and Stephanie, and she visited the model home site on the same day they did. It struck me as too coincidental."

"I'll make sure we talk with her first. Why don't you go home and get some rest? The last time I saw you, you didn't look all that good."

"Well, thanks a heap." I pulled down the mirrored visor and looked at myself. He had a point.

There was a definite pregnant pause. "May, I have to say this. You're off the case, Brenda is my partner, and you and I shouldn't be having these conversations. I don't want to get in trouble over this. We're having to re-investigate people you and I already talked to, because you aren't officially a part of this."

I knew this was coming but it still felt like I'd been gut-punched. "You know I don't want to hinder this case or cause you trouble. But how do I just walk away, Ed? Tell me how to do that and I will."

"You and I both know you won't. Only call me on my cell, and do the same with Janet. She's in the same fix I am. That way, we can keep in touch with you. I don't want you out there alone, but I know anything I say won't stop you. You're too hard-headed and you loved this guy."

"Like a father."

"Yeah, whatever you say. By the way, some lawyer called you about a dozen times. Did you get the messages?"

"If it was Rick Purdue, I returned his call. Maybe he left a message at the house, since I left my number. I think maybe those people who bought my house in Tacoma finally noticed the roof leaks."

"That should have been disclosed when you sold the property, May. How could they not know that?"

"Because when they bought it the sun was shining and the roof wasn't leaking, silly."

"You're going to need a lawyer to get out of this mess. Go home, May. Rest and sleep. I'll keep in touch and you do the same. And no more prowling around Las Vegas."

"I promise. I know you had to say what you did, even if I didn't want to hear it. I'll only call you and Janet on the cell."

# Seven

For once I did what he said and slept. In fact, I slept most of the next day and was horrified when I finally looked at the clock and it was almost noon. I thought the clock was ringing and it was time to get up and go to work, but it was the telephone.

I knocked the clock off the table and fell out of bed trying to reach the phone. Finally, in a tangle of covers and a sleeping cat, I answered.

"Hello?"

"This is Rick Purdue. Am I speaking with May Scott?"

"Yes, this is May Scott, and you can tell those owners they should've had the house inspected before they bought it. I even left the buckets in the attic so when they went up there they'd see them. Otherwise, why would I have buckets sitting all over the floor? Common sense would tell you the roof leaks." There was a definite quiet on the other end of the line. "Hello? Are you still there?" I asked, certain the connection had been lost.

"Yes, I'm here. I gather you think this is about the sale of a property, Miss Scott?"

"Well, what else could it be?" I got up off the floor and sat on the edge of the bed.

"The law firm of Bush, Catrel, and Smith in Tacoma, Washington, requested that we contact you for the reading of the will of Mr. Harvey Jordan. Can you be at our law offices at two this afternoon?"

"Will? Why do I need to hear about Harvey's will?"

"Can you be here today at two?"

"Yes, where did you say you were located?" Whiskers sleepwalked onto my lap and purred as I stroked her soft black fur.

He gave the address, which was in Summerlin, the high rent district of Las Vegas.

After he hung up, I held the phone in my hand and stared at it. I disliked attorneys and most certainly didn't want to hear anything about Harvey's will. But, I was intrigued and decided there might be something Rick Purdue could tell me about Harvey, Stephanie, and the murder. I untangled myself from the covers, the cat, and headed for the shower.

By the time I'd cleaned up, dressed, fed Whiskers, and listened to a few more of my messages it was time to leave for the law office.

The drive to Summerlin didn't take long. The law office was located in a new building. Since most of the building was made of glass, it sparkled in the warm Nevada sun. As I took the escalator to the second floor, the valley circled by snow-capped caramel-colored mountains, was awe-inspiring through the glass-paneled building. The surrounding high desert country was spectacular. To the west, the reddish-orange mountains of Red Rock Canyon glowed like they were on fire.

I got off the escalator and walked down a hallway toward the tall double doors of the law offices of Purdue, Wesson & Jeffries. Their names were written in elegant, small gold script. I opened the door. Ivory-colored carpet extended through the waiting area and sleek marble floors flowed toward the offices. Glass sculptures in hues of green and blue sat on several tabletops. I was trying to remember that phrase about glass houses and rocks when the receptionist asked if she could help me.

"I'm May Scott and have an appointment with Mr. Purdue."

"Yes, Miss Scott. He's waiting for you. Let me show you where his office is located."

I couldn't help but compare the swishing backside of this young woman to Diana/Dickie. "He's right at the end of this hall," she indicated then she returned to her desk in the waiting area.

I walked down the pale green-colored hall. As I approached he opened the door and held out his hand. "It's nice to finally meet you in person, May. I hope it's all right to call you May or would you prefer Detective Scott?" he smiled and his tanned cheeks dimpled.

I shook his hand. "May is fine."

"And please, call me Rick." He was younger than I thought he'd be and very attractive. His dark hair was cut in a boyish style and it flopped onto his forehead. As with most lawyers, he wore a tailored, conservative dark suit and the watch on his wrist looked like a Rolex.

He motioned for me to sit in a beautifully upholstered green chair while he walked around his large oak desk and sat down in his bone-colored leather chair. "I wish we could be meeting under different circumstances. I know this is an especially trying time for you." His blue eyes looked at me with kindness.

"I lost my Dad a little while back, and I think I can understand the pain you must be feeling now. From my understanding, Harvey Jordan considered you to be his daughter."

"Yes, he was like a father to me. I mean, I had a dad, but he died when I was very young. I was raised by my grandpa."

He smiled and lifted a file that was on top of his desk. "I'll read his will to you and a lot of it'll be in legal jargon. But to get to the point of our meeting, Harvey left you all of his assets, which as it turns out, are considerable. He was a very wealthy man. He and his wife, Stephanie, set up their wills so her children would inherit from her estate and you would receive his. You are, according to Harvey, his beloved daughter by choice, not circumstance, and the sole heir of his estate."

When he said that, tears streamed down my face and I couldn't stop them. He handed me a box of tissues and I wiped the tears away. "I know I need to get myself under control, but I loved him so much."

"I'm going to leave you for awhile. If you still aren't ready, take all the time you need."

His voice was soft, his blue eyes were kind and with a few words my world had changed.

He left me alone for a few minutes and it gave me time to sort through my emotions and get myself under control. When he came back, I had an immediate question.

"How can this be done so fast? I thought wills dragged on forever."

"They can, but in this case, part of the will was to let you know about this within twenty-four hours of his death."

"Why?"

"We'll get to that in a few minutes. Do you think you're ready to go through this now or do you need more time?"

"I'm ready," I said as tears continued to snake their way down my face. I thought I had cried away all the tears, but there seemed to be an endless supply. If this was grief, then I understood how a person could be crippled with pain. Every part of me hurt. I felt like a raw wound.

Rick didn't lie. I didn't understand most of the will, especially the real estate descriptions. It was a good thing he was there to translate for me. What it amounted to was that I got everything that belonged to Harvey. I'd known that he was good with money. I just had no idea he was also good with stocks, bonds, real estate, insurance and mutual funds. It was too much to take in. I sat back in the plush chair when Rick finished. "I'd rather have Harvey in my life than all of his money and property."

"I know that, May. But he wanted to take care of you because he loved you so much. You won't ever have to work another day in your life if you don't want to."

"I've worked my whole life. In fact, my life has been about work. I don't have much else in it, but a cat."

"I'll file this with probate, May, but there is one more item I need to stress. I don't know if you picked up on this or not, but there's a safe deposit box in a bank vault in Tacoma that Harvey wanted you to be sure and open within the first few days after his death. 'As soon as she can get to Tacoma,' is what he stipulated. I have all of the information here that you'll need in order to open it. If you would like, I'll book you on the next flight to Washington. Unless, of course, you want to go out and buy your own plane."

He smiled when he said this, but it was true. I could buy anything I wanted. The thing was, all I wanted was for Harvey and Stephanie to be alive and part of my life. I laid my head on my arms on his desk. I couldn't deal with one more thing.

I hired Rick as my attorney and he promised to translate the will into understandable English. It was overwhelming that less than two hours ago I could barely get my bills paid and now I was wealthy. Exactly how rich, I would know as soon as Rick had done his homework. For someone who didn't like lawyers, I'd certainly fallen under his spell.

I left the law office, got into my car and drove home in a daze. As soon as I pulled into my driveway, I looked for Whiskers. I was surprised when she wasn't in her normal place on the windowsill. I gathered the papers I'd been given by the law staff and got out of the car, making sure I locked the door.

As I walked toward my house, I fumbled in my purse for my key, but found the front door ajar. Since I automatically lock doors, I was amazed that I'd left it like that. I nudged it open and found a mess. The part of the house that I could see had been ransacked. Tables were overturned, my grandmother's lamps were shattered, and papers scattered everywhere. I pulled my gun from the holster that was in the back of my suit jacket and took a tentative step inside.

Something slammed down onto the top of my head and the pain made me see stars.

I woke to the sound of Whiskers meowing at me and her cold nose rubbed against mine. I tried to sit up but couldn't. I dragged myself over to the phone, which had been knocked to the floor, picked it up, and called Ed's cell. By some miracle, he answered.

"Ed, I've been attacked at my house. I'm hurt. Please help me."

After saying that, I passed out. The next things I remember are flashing lights, a stretcher and sirens.

After what seemed only a few minutes, I opened my eyes. They felt swollen. Everything around me was blindingly white and there were tubes running out of me in all directions. Ed was sitting on a chair near the bed and I called his name, but realized my voice was too weak for him to hear me. He had his eyes closed and I thought he was asleep.

I called his name again and he looked at me. The look in his eyes told me how close I'd come to joining Harvey and Stephanie.

"My prayers have been answered," he said.

For the next few days, I stayed in that austere hospital room, vowing never again to paint any room I lived in white. My house was now a crime scene and Janet had lots of fun telling me how she got to go through all of my things in her search for evidence. She'd taken Whiskers home to stay with her and Frankie until I got out of the hospital.

My two constant visitors were Ed and Rick, who disliked each other from the moment they met.

# Eight

"Janet, please stop mother-henning me. You're driving me crazy," I complained, as she once more plumped the pillows behind my head.

"You need to heal and if you knew how sick you really looked, you wouldn't be giving me grief about this. Now behave yourself and stay put. I've got to go to work, but here's the phone, the TV remote, and Whiskers is somewhere in the house; so you're set. Frankie will stop by at noon to get your lunch for you, so don't you move. Do you hear me? The only reason I want you out of bed is to go to the bathroom. Everything else is off limits." With that, Janet gave me a kiss on the forehead, patted my hand, and left in a swirl of motion.

Her house was so quiet. I didn't like all the silence, so I got up to find Whiskers. Both of us had moved in with Janet and Frankie, at her insistence. It was a good idea, but I was fed up with being treated like an invalid. I mean, it was only a bump on the head four whole days ago, but the only way they would release me from the hospital was if I had a place to go where I would be taken care of and monitored.

Janet jumped at the chance to mother me, since she had been doing it for more years than I cared to remember. I love Janet, I really do. But this invalid stuff wasn't setting well. Enough, as they say, is enough.

I slid off the high bed and my feet hit the floor with a thump. I steadied myself on the edge of the bed, and took a few tentative steps to see what would happen. I was pleased that I was doing just fine, so maybe this patient crap would end sooner than anyone expected. I carefully walked toward the kitchen and called for Whiskers.

She came out from under Janet's sofa where she liked to hide. She could keep track of all the action, but stay out of sight that way. We went into the kitchen and I gave her fresh food and water, then scooped her up and petted her. I felt a bit dizzy when I bent over to pick her up, but it passed quickly. I sat Whiskers on the counter until I got my equilibrium back. Janet didn't like her on her kitchen counters, so I put her back on the floor.

Janet was a wonderful friend and I trusted her absolutely with everything. She and Harvey were the two people in my life who knew everything about me and loved me anyway.

Janet's comment about how I looked intrigued me, so I decided to see for myself. I walked into the bathroom, turned on the light, and stared at the shrunken woman with dark-circled eyes, and a suspicious brown color showing at the root line of her red hair. Janet had pegged it. I looked like road kill. It was a long way from how I'd looked when I'd been the Homecoming Queen back in Montana. The person in the mirror definitely wouldn't win any crowns.

I went back into the bedroom and called Ed. He answered on the first ring, which pleased me.

"Ed? This is me."

"How is 'me' doing today? Are you staying in bed like the doctors told you to do? You know, if you don't, they'll put you right back in the hospital. Personally, I don't think they should have let you out in the first place. You aren't going to listen to them, are you? What are you up to?" my partner, who knew me too well, asked.

"I'm following each and every rule. I always do everything everybody tells me to do. You know that, Ed."

There was total silence on the other end of the line.

Finally, he said, "That's such a stupid comment; I don't even know what to say. Now, what's going on?"

"Are you mad at me?" I tried to sound innocent.

"No, not yet. Should I be mad at you, May?"

"No, but you sound crabbier than usual. So, if you're not mad at me are you coming to visit today?"

"You know I will. I visit you everyday, don't I?"

"Yes."

"So, what's up?"

"Could you stop by the pharmacy and buy me some hair color?"
He gave a big sigh. "What color do you want?"

"'Persimmon Surprise'. Just ask one of the sales clerks, they'll
show you where it's located. You can tell me what's going on with
Harvey and Stephanie's case, too. I feel like I'm out of the loop."

"You should be out of this loop, May, for many reasons. I'll come
over within the hour. Keep the door locked. Do you hear me? Don't
open it for anybody but Janet, Frankie or me. Do you get that?"

"Yes. Wait a minute, how about Rick? Can I open the door for
Rick?"

"No!"

"Why do you dislike him so much? He's been wonderful to me."

"Because he's a well-dressed, good looking dirt bag. He gives me
the creeps. In fact, I'm having a background check run on him."

"You must be nuts. He's the main partner in a big Summerlin law
firm. Why in the world are you having him checked out?" I asked,
my aggravation growing by the minute.

"Let's put it this way. I thought Ernie was bad, but he's a choirboy
compared to this bozo. Your taste in men is terrible. Take my word
for it you don't want this loser anywhere around you. I'm telling you
this for your own good. Now listen to me and don't open that door
for anyone but me, Janet or Frankie. Period!"

"Okay, I won't open the door, but you're wrong about Rick."

When Ed arrived I unlocked the door and let him in. "You look
awful. You do need this stuff, don't you?" He handed me the box of
hair color.

"Yeah, I know. Actually, I don't feel that bad, just a little dizzy
sometimes," I commented as I took the box into the bathroom. "Do
you want some coffee? I just put a pot together."

"Sure, why not? You make great coffee and you're a good cook
when you take time to do it. See? I'm not being crabby, I'm being

nice." He smiled. "I'm glad you're doing better. I don't know what I'd do if you hadn't made it. I've lost too many partners over the years."

It's a good thing I was busy with coffee cups, cream and sugar, otherwise I might've started crying again. It was rare, but sometimes Ed did let his guard down. He didn't talk about the two partners who'd been killed in the line of duty. I'd told him he should, but he couldn't do it.

"It's not like what you went through before. I'm doing great. Do you want to talk about Tim and Jeff?"

"No! I'm just glad you're okay. I will tell you that Brenda's doing a good job. You've got to get over being jealous of her. She's a nice young woman. Probably a lot like you were at that age."

He was stating facts as he knew them and didn't know his comments hurt my feelings. I didn't feel old or sick, even if I had just been released from the hospital. I wondered if the blow to my head had done more than I suspected. And then there was the will that I hadn't told anyone about. Not Ed or Janet, no one but Rick knew about that.

"Hello? Earth to May? Are you out there in the cosmos somewhere?"

I looked at him, smiled, and poured his coffee. In a weird, platonic way we loved each other. His wife knew all about it and didn't mind.

The case hadn't progressed very far. The car I spotted up at the development had been a rental, as were most of the cars in Las Vegas. The man who'd rented it swore he hadn't driven it after he'd parked it in the huge Mandalay Bay Hotel garage. The mileage, however, didn't show that; someone had driven the car.

The forensics teams took the car back to their facility on the outskirts of Las Vegas and were giving the car a complete search. Janet was monitoring it so I knew that when and if something was found I'd know. Ed and I talked for about an hour and then he left to go back to work. I knew he could get into trouble for talking to me about the case, but I'd have done the same for him, if our positions had been switched.

My gut told me that whoever I saw that night was the killer and was the same person who'd tried to kill me. What I didn't understand, though, was why? What was the connection? Was it someone who was angry that Harvey had left everything to me, such as a disgruntled family member? I certainly hadn't met everyone in Harvey or Stephanie's family, but those I had met didn't seem to be the murdering sort. But then when it came to a large inheritance, anything could happen. Questions swirled in my head. I lay down for a while to think things through. Of course, as soon as my head hit the pillow, I was out. The drugs I'd taken didn't let me stay awake for long.

# Nine

"Wake up, Aunt May. It's time for your lunch."

"Who's it?" I mumbled, still half asleep, but my nose twitched, as I smelled something enticing. "Smells good. Frankie? You cook lunch?"

"Yes, Aunt May, let's sit you up. I have some soup that Mom left for you. She made it last night while you were sleeping. It's great – it has all this healthy crap in it, but it tastes good. You'll like it."

Frankie helped prop me up so I could sample the soup. He was the light of Janet's life, and mine, too, if I thought real hard about it. Being childless, Frankie had become my adopted son; Janet didn't mind.

The soup was wonderful and Janet had baked bread. Frankie slathered more butter on it than I usually eat in a month. I ate until I couldn't put one more bite in my mouth.

"You did good, Aunt May. I think this will help you get better real soon. Do you need anything else before I go back to school?"

"No, I'm fine. Thanks for taking such good care of me."

He smiled. "My pleasure. You're 'Number Two.' Remember how I used to call you that when you babysat me?"

"It seems like yesterday. How in the world did you grow up so quickly?"

"Living with the two of you; a forensic scientist mom and a homicide detective aunt can make you grow up fast. How many crime scenes do you think I've been to over the years? I've spent more time in the morgue than a dead person," he laughed.

"Well, at least I can understand why you decided you wanted to

51

become a doctor."

"But for people who are alive, not like the ones you and Mom work with all the time."

"I see your point. You go on back to school. I love you, you know," I smiled at him.

"I know. I just wish Kim loved me."

"Who's Kim?" I asked, all ears.

"This luscious babe in my calculus class. She's beautiful, smart, and built like a…well, you get the picture. She doesn't know I exist."

"Why don't you ask her out?"

"Me? Are you kidding? She'd laugh."

"Frankie, do you know what a smart hunk you are? Go look in the mirror, kid. You've got the best parts of your handsome, fighter pilot dad and your brainy scientist mom."

Frankie laughed. "I don't think of myself like that."

"You should. I tell you what. Ask Kim out and I'll pay for your date – anywhere you want to take her."

"You? You don't have any money, Aunt May. I'd really like to take her to the Stratosphere. It's way cool up there. But it's expensive."

"I'm telling you, guy, your Auntie will give you the world. Ask Kim to go with you to the Stratosphere for dinner and dancing. If you want, you can go in a limo," I tossed in at the last minute.

"Sure, and you'll spend the afternoon robbing a bank, huh?"

"Old Auntie has her ways. Go ask her out. This afternoon. Time's-a-wasting."

He was shaking his head and laughing on the way out the door. I hoped he'd get up the courage to ask the lovely Kim out on a date.

It was beginning to dawn on me just what kinds of things I could do… now that I was a rich woman. This might turn into a good thing.

I spent the rest of the afternoon trying to improve my appearance. Being old was for the birds. I was in the prime of my life and getting back my red hair was a step in that direction. Carefully, I worked around my wound and colored just the new hair growth. It felt good to take a warm shower and wash my hair. After I finished, I applied make-up or as Ed called it, war paint. I dug around in the clothes that

Janet had brought from my house and put on my favorite turquoise top. It was a little too tight, but with my black jeans, I looked smashing.

Because I felt so much better I called Rick, in spite of Ed's warning to stay clear of him. He, too, had been stopping by on a regular basis and today I'd receive the easy-to-understand translation of the will. I still couldn't believe Harvey had done this for me. But I was starting to realize the enormity of how it could change my life and the lives of those I loved.

Rick showed up within thirty minutes after leaving his office because he had to deal with cross-town traffic. Janet's house was near Nellis Air Force Base. Her estranged husband, Major Tom McHenry, was a pilot stationed at Nellis. I'd thought the two of them would get back together. Neither expressed any interest in other people over the years and they'd never divorced. At least it'd been good for Frankie, having his dad close by and it was kind of cool to have a dad who flew jets. Tom had turned down promotions to stay near Janet and Frankie and, in my mind, that was unusual for a military man. I'd always liked him and hoped one day they'd get back together.

The bell rang and I opened the door. "You look great," Rick said. "What've you done to yourself? The last time I saw you, you could hardly get out of bed and now you look, well, you look…"

"Yes?" I asked hopefully.

"Healthier."

We stood there, in Janet's hall, and I took a deep breath. "So, you have the will sorted out for me?"

He put his briefcase on the table, opened it and took out a thick booklet. "Here it is, and the estimated amount of what you'll have available from the estate. You know, Harvey invested in a lot of real estate over the years. Were you aware of that?"

"I heard him talk about it, but I wasn't interested. He used to teach a class at the local community college about investing, stocks and bonds, real estate, mutual funds, insurance and retirement funding. I signed up for it a couple of times, but got so bored I always left during the first session."

"I hope his other students listened to him because he didn't miss a beat when it came to making money. He should've been a financial advisor instead of a cop."

"Harvey was the most important person in my life. I learned so much from him but none of it was about money."

"I want to remind you that you have to fly to Tacoma and open that safety deposit box. There's no telling what might be in there."

We walked into the living room and sat down on the couch. "I know. I haven't forgotten about that and I'll get around to it. Would you like something to drink?"

"I'd like an orange juice if you think Janet won't mind."

"No, I'm sure she wouldn't mind. And I intend to pay her back for all of this nursing she's done for me. Speaking of that, could you explain how I go about drawing money from the estate? I promised Frankie that I'd pay for a night on the town for him and his girlfriend."

Rick followed me into the kitchen and explained what I would need to do as I poured his juice. While Rick talked about wills, probate and all that legal stuff, I noticed he smelled nice. "What's that cologne you're wearing? You smell great."

He laughed and said he wasn't sure. "I grab whatever bottle is nearest to me in the morning."

He finished his drink, said he had to go, and left.

I was mulling over another shower, this one cold, when the phone rang. I picked it up, and before I could say hello, heard a disguised voice say:

"Meet me at the gravesite tonight at eleven. If you bring anybody with you or tell anybody about this, I'll kill the woman and her kid."

The phone went dead. The killer knew where I was; he was tracking me. Janet and Frankie were in danger and I wasn't sure I was strong enough to handle this alone. I hit review to find the number he'd called from but it rang endlessly. It was probably a pay phone. I sat down on the couch where Rick had been a few minutes earlier and prayed for guidance on what I should do next.

# Ten

It didn't take long to figure out that I needed a car. At first, I thought I'd call a cab, but figured I'd have more control if I were driving. I went into the kitchen, found the big information directory and looked under the rental car section. Several of the agencies would bring the car to me which in this case was necessary. I wouldn't need it for long, but I wanted to go to my house, primarily to get my gun.

Within an hour, the car had been delivered and I was preparing to return to my house. Janet had told me the crime scene tape was still up, but that they'd finished the forensics. I should get out of Janet and Frankie's lives as soon as possible, now that the killer was stalking me.

Before I left Janet's, I wrote her a note and told her I'd call later with details. I asked that she keep Whiskers until I found myself another place to live. I didn't want to go back to my house, but I needed to pick up a few items. I now understood why crime victims often moved away after a robbery or assault in their home. Somehow, it didn't seem like it was my house anymore and I didn't feel safe. I packed a bag with the clothes Janet had brought, petted Whiskers and left.

The drive to my house took longer than planned. There'd been an accident and roads were blocked in all directions. I finally pulled into a shopping area and parked the car. I watched for suspicious movement, cars, and people, but nothing seemed out of the ordinary. I pulled my cell phone out of my purse and called Ed. He wasn't in, so I left a message for him to call as quickly as he could. This time, I needed my partner desperately. I wanted his advice on how to handle the threat to Janet and Frankie.

I sat there until traffic cleared, then I pulled back onto the highway. The rest of the drive was uneventful and I eventually pulled into my driveway. It was sad to see yellow crime scene tape decorating my yard. The front door had a large, 'Do Not Enter – Las Vegas Metro Police' sign, and was padlocked. I walked around the house and, as I figured, there was no lock on the back door. I couldn't wait to complain to someone about this procedural mistake. I opened the door with my key and entered what used to be my home. It didn't look like it had the last time I was here or at least the time I could remember. It was a complete mess.

For all of my problems, keeping a neat house has never been one of them. I get nervous if things aren't orderly. That amazed Janet, who tended to be a bit sloppy when it came to housekeeping chores. It reminded me that I had to decide quickly how to handle the threat to Janet and Frankie. I thought about it, then looked up and dialed Major McHenry's number at Nellis Air Force Base.

"Major McHenry," he answered.

"Major, this is May Scott. I'm surprised you actually answered on the first ring."

"It's good to hear from you. I'm finishing paperwork I've put off for as long as I can. I can't tell you how I hate this stuff."

"Believe me; I know exactly how you feel. Listen, I don't want to keep you away from work, but I do have something serious to talk over with you. It concerns Janet and Frankie."

"Are they alright?" he asked, concern in his voice.

"Yes, for now, but I'm going to need your help."

I explained the situation and he agreed that Janet and Frankie shouldn't go back to their house, at least for a day or two.

"Do you think I should call Janet or do you want to do it?" I asked.

"I'll do it," he said. "Janet and I are having dinner together tonight anyway and Frankie is staying with one of his buddies. I don't think it'll be too much of a stretch to get Janet to come back to the base with me," he said. "We can throw some clothes in a bag, call Frankie and tell him to come to my place after school tomorrow. It'll work out fine, May. Just take care of yourself. Do you really think this guy is serious and would hurt Janet and Frankie?"

"Yes, there are two dead bodies in the morgue right now. This person is definitely crazy serious, Major."

"I feel like I should do something else to help you. How about if I fly over tonight in my F-16?"

"That would really be great, but I don't think the Air Force would appreciate getting mixed up in a local murder investigation."

"Yeah, you're right. I just want to do something to help."

"You're doing an immense thing for me – you're going to take care of my best girlfriend and Frankie."

"You've got it. I'll call tonight and give you an update, but I don't expect any problems with my end of the operation."

We said quick goodbyes and I'd just closed the cell phone when it rang again. Being certain who it was I said, "Ed?"

"No, this is Brenda Mitchell returning your call. Ed asked that I take his calls this afternoon. How are you doing, May? We're all pulling for you."

I couldn't believe this. Of all the people I didn't want to talk to, Brenda Mitchell was near the top of the list.

"I'm doing fine, Brenda. When will Ed be available?"

"He went to the dentist. He's been avoiding it for weeks, but the pain got so bad he had to go. I've never seen a grown man so scared of going to the dentist." I could tell she was smiling.

"He won't be back in today, I gather?"

"Probably not. I think the pain pills will knock him out after he leaves the dentist. What can I do for you, May?"

I heard the sincerity in her voice and it made me feel terrible. Why did I dislike this young woman so much? What was it about Brenda that set me on such an edge? I needed to make an attitude adjustment. "Just have Ed call when he gets a chance. Let's you and I get together soon and have lunch. Ed told me that you're great to work with and he thinks very highly of you."

"Oh, that's so wonderful to hear. I know he misses you; he talks about you all the time. I've tried hard to do a good job. Thanks for telling me that."

We said goodbye and I put my phone back into my purse.

"Now what?" I moaned.

# Eleven

I had to find a place to stay but first I wanted to talk with Mrs. Bride again. She was the only witness so far who'd seen Harvey and Stephanie before they'd been murdered. That meant a trip to Caesar's Palace. I gathered up my gun, more clothes, and cosmetics to add to the few Janet had brought me. I walked around the house and looked in dismay at what had been destroyed, probably on purpose. He might have been looking for something, but I had no idea what that might be.

I locked up the house, left the rental car for courtesy pick-up, and drove my car onto the Strip. At this time of the day it was jammed so I prepared to sit and wait more than move forward. Eventually I got to the turn in for Caesar's Palace and drove into their underground parking garage. Since I wasn't in an official car, I couldn't take advantage of the reserved parking for police vehicles. Luckily, I found a place that was fairly close to the elevators. After taking the elevator from the garage, I had to go into the lobby area to get another elevator that led to the 35th floor.

The doors opened silently and I stepped into the long hallway that I'd been in a few days ago. So much had happened it seemed like years since I'd stood outside of Mrs. Bride's room. As I was about to knock, the door of the room next to Mrs. Bride, on the other side from where Harvey and Stephanie had stayed, opened. A tall, slender woman walked out, saw me, smiled, and then walked in the direction of the elevators.

"Excuse me," I called.

59

"Yes?" she said as she turned around.

"My name is Detective May Scott, Las Vegas Metro Police. Are you Anne Lambert, by any chance?" I pulled out my badge and held it in front of her.

"Yes, I am. I remember you left a note with your card. I didn't have any information, so I didn't call. It's sad about that couple. Have you found out who did it yet?"

"It's an ongoing police investigation so I'm not at liberty to say," I replied, right from the rulebook.

"Yes, I know that sort of lingo. I'm the Medical Examiner for Reno. Were you aware of that?"

"No, I'm afraid I didn't know. I've been out of the loop for a few days. Were you here for the Police Convention?" I put my badge in my purse.

"Yes, in fact, I presented two sessions on forensics. I enjoy lecturing. So anytime I'm asked I go, if my schedule permits. I was on my way to have something to eat. Would you care to join me?" Anne asked.

"I'd enjoy that," I replied, thinking what an attractive woman she was, tall and slim. Sexy, stiletto heels covered her small elegant feet. She was probably a brunette under that long blond hair, since her eyes were dark-brown, about the same color as mine. She towered over me, which isn't that hard to do since I'm only 5'1", and on good days, weigh about 100 pounds. I was barely large enough to qualify for the police department, but I made up for it in attitude.

Anne and I went down to the main floor and decided on a restaurant in the Forum Shops area. There was constant noise from the casino and tourists as they walked along the remarkably realistic Roman streets.

"For some reason, Anne, your name sounds familiar to me. Have we met somewhere or have you written a book about forensics I might've read?"

"Maybe we have met. But my name, Anne Lambert, is fairly common. I haven't written a book. I'm too busy in the lab and the field to do that."

"I can see how that would be possible. You mentioned that you work in Reno. Have you been there long?" I hoped I wouldn't insult her, since she knew I was as politely as possible questioning her.

"I've been there five years. Before that, I was in windy Chicago."

The waiter came to take our order and I had another chance to watch this fascinating woman. I should take a class from her in how to sit, dress, do hair, makeup, and talk with waiters. She had him eating out of her hand within minutes. I was beginning to feel like the poor little country mouse.

"Did you enjoy working in Chicago?" I asked, still wondering why her name sounded familiar. Then a light dawned. "Of course, I heard Harvey Jordan talk about you. He and I worked together in Tacoma before he took a job with the Chicago Police Department. He mentioned how much you helped with his cases."

"Yes, he was a great guy. I couldn't believe it when I read in the paper that he and his wife had been murdered. Do you have any good leads?"

"To tell you the truth, I got thrown off the case because the lieutenant thought I was too close to it. So, I'm actually on leave with orders not to intrude on the two detectives who are working it. To answer your question, I have no idea. I'm being left out of the loop."

"That must be driving you crazy. I remember Harvey talked about the detective he worked with in Tacoma. That was you, huh? I always figured you two were lovers," she said, stirring her daiquiri with a straw.

"No. Everybody made the wrong assumption about Harvey and me. He was the father I'd lost and I was the daughter he never had."

"Are you sure? I think you meant more to him than a daughter."

"I'm positive of who I was to Harvey and who he was to me," I replied, becoming annoyed.

She seemed to pick up on my irritation because she backed off in a hurry and went on to other safer topics. She really was an interesting woman and once I'd corralled my temper, we had an enjoyable time.

It never left my mind that I had many things to do before I went up to the housing development to meet the killer. I had a half-formed plan in my head, but I was going to need backup and I knew exactly who could help me pull it off. And when Ed found out, he'd skin me alive. Also, if I could squeeze it in, I wanted to talk with Mrs. Bride.

Since I had no place to spend the next few days I decided that this hotel, which was my favorite anyway, would do just fine. On my way to the registration desk I walked through the casino, past Cleopatra's Barge. The first time I'd seen it, Cleopatra had been on board serving drinks to a barge full of tourists. She wasn't in evidence tonight, but it didn't seem to matter. The tourists looked happy as they sipped their drinks, served by scantily clad women in Roman garb. The barge, supposedly floating on the Nile, was anchored firmly so tourists wouldn't fall overboard into the water.

The casino was filled with people, as it is twenty-four hours a day, seven days a week. There are never windows or clocks in any casino. They don't want the players to know what time it is or whether it's day or night. It's always the right time to gamble in Las Vegas. People were dressed in all manner of outfits, from sloppy to evening dress. Smoking is allowed in the casinos, but the filtering system is so good that it's not overwhelming, even to a non-smoker like me. All the employees were dressed in various costumes to support the Caesar and Cleopatra theme.

I'd thought that when I retired I might work for one of the casinos. My pension would be too small to support me without some sort of extra income. Now that wasn't going to be necessary. Unless, of course, I just wanted to do it for fun.

As I approached the registration desk I saw that Mel was on duty. "Hi, Mel. Remember me?"

He looked at me in total puzzlement. "Uh, no, I'm afraid I don't. Are you a guest?"

"Not yet but I would like to have a room, please. Anywhere but the 35th floor." I couldn't deal with being on the floor where Harvey and Stephanie had stayed.

"Here's my credit card." I handed it over to Mel and wondered if I'd have enough money to cover the bill. Then I remembered. I was rich. My whole life had been about living on the financial edge and now I was wealthy. I'd have to make another attitude adjustment.

Mel had me fill out way too much paperwork but I did it as quickly as possible. I needed to get my plan, which in no way resembled correct police procedure, in motion. Ed was right. I wasn't very good at the part of being a police officer that involved making and following rules. Black and white is not my world. My world is a perpetual shade of foggy-gray.

I thanked Mel and left the desk with my key envelope clutched in my hand. I was on the 9th floor and I found the room quickly. I made it into the room without having to call someone to help me get the key system to work. I know hotels are security conscious, but I would hate to have to open one of these doors if someone was after me. When I thought of that, I quickly scanned up and down the long quiet hallway. My imagination was in overdrive.

The room was nice, but not as large as Harvey and Stephanie's. The bathroom was the size of my living room and had one of those wonderful spa tubs. I sincerely hoped I would live long enough to use it.

I went to the phone, picked it up, and called Ernie.

"Hello?" Nora answered. She was his latest live-in. I liked her much more than some of the other women Ernie had lived with. He'd tried to talk me into moving in with him but I'd always resisted. I enjoyed living alone and having my own place. Also, Ernie just wasn't the type of man I'd want to live with. He was, though, a good friend to have when you were in a jam.

"Hi, Nora, this is May. Is Ernie there?"

"Well, hello, May. I haven't heard your voice in a long time. Let me get him for you. I was so sorry to hear about your friends' deaths and then you getting attacked. Ernie was very, very upset over that. If I didn't know better I might be jealous of you," she laughed. "Let me get him, just a second."

"May, it's great to hear from you," Ernie said.

"I need your help."

"No problem. What's up?"

"I need you and some of your motorcycle buddies to help pull something off. Here's what I have in mind." I told him about the threatening call and the plan I'd cooked up.

He agreed to help, but still asked, "Does the lieutenant or Ed know about this?"

"No."

"I knew the answer to that before I asked," he chuckled.

When he put his mind to it, Ernie was the best motorcycle cop in Las Vegas. He also belonged to a biker club. They rode all over the desert at least twice a month. Every year he rode his huge bike to Sturgis, South Dakota, where the Harley riders gather. That's also where he'd found several of his live-ins, including Nora.

"Ernie, I'll never forget you for this one. Could you do one more thing for me and give me the name of your friend who flies helicopters? You know the guy I mean; he flies tourists over Hoover Dam and the Grand Canyon."

"Sure. His name is David Greer. He not only flies copters, he's in the Reserves and works at Indian Springs Air Force Base. I'll give you his number."

After talking to Ernie, I felt better. At least now I wouldn't be alone on top of the mountain with a killer who had my name on his list, and had added Janet and Frankie.

A little past nine, I called David Greer and arranged for him to fly over the site at eleven. With the helicopter searchlights sweeping the area, my goal was to force the killer out into the open. Between the roar of Ernie's cycle buddies and the helicopter, it would get noisy and bright on top of the mountain. It would be hard for the killer to hide.

I changed out of my turquoise top into a black hooded sweatshirt. I knew the killer could use a gun at point blank range. I hoped his distance shooting wouldn't be as accurate.

I took one last look around the room, gazed longingly at the spa tub, then left. The elevator ride was interesting. I shared it with a couple that was on their way to be married. She had on a beautiful wedding dress complete with a veil and the groom had on a white tuxedo. They looked like they were the decorations on top of a wedding cake.

When the doors of the elevator opened the bride said, "We have to hurry, the limo is waiting for us." With that, they ran through the lobby. People stopped in their tracks to watch the attractive couple, the bride's fairy-tale gown and veil billowed behind her, as they ran full tilt toward the front doors of Caesar's Palace. People smiled and applauded, cameras flashed and I thought, *Only in Las Vegas*. You never know what's going to be around the next corner.

I walked to my car in the parking garage, unlocked it, and started the engine. I was going to be early for the meeting. If things went as planned the killer would be in my custody in less than two hours. If traffic was reasonable and it usually was this time of the night, I should arrive at the gravesite by ten.

I arrived early, called Ed and his wife answered. As I suspected, the dentist's painkillers knocked him out. I asked Barbara to tell him I'd called. I promised myself to tell him what I'd done as soon as he was back to normal. I knew he wouldn't approve but I wanted him to know the truth about how I'd handled the situation. It would have a happy ending because in less than an hour I'd have the killer in custody.

I parked behind the sales office and sat in my car for a few minutes to get used to the dark. I made sure the inside light was turned off so no one would see me when I opened the door. It was very dark and quiet on top of the mountain. Somewhere close by a dog barked and it sounded lonesome. Even though the Strip was only minutes away I felt completely isolated up here. The sky was star filled and the moon resembled a keyhole to the universe. I felt inside my pocket for my gun. It felt cold and wonderful. I've always loved guns.

My grandfather, who raised me after my parents died, worshiped the ground I walked on. I was a lifesaver for him, too, because my grandmother had died the year before. It was terrible that he'd lost her and his only son within one year of each other.

He taught me all he knew about guns and hunting. We'd walked the long empty stretches of the Montana plains during each hunting season, looking for whatever animal or bird was in season. He and I consoled each other and brought joy back into each other's lives. When he died I was seventeen, Frankie's age. I smiled when I thought of him. He'd worn denim overalls, smoked a pipe and smelled of rich tobacco and his beloved hunting dogs.

To this day, if I smell a pipe, I follow my nose to the source. I've loved three men in my life who loved me back, and each of them left me. I looked up into the starry Nevada sky and wondered if they were watching me from somewhere in the cosmos. I hoped they were proud of me because I still loved them with all my heart.

I got out of the car, quietly closed the door and moved in close to the building. I crept along the back, behind the bushes, hoping to stay out of sight. There were several cars sitting in the large parking area, but most of them looked like company vehicles for the development. So far, I didn't see or hear anything out of the ordinary. Diana's area was dark, but then I wasn't surprised. Diana had become Dickie by now and was busy captivating his audience at the Choices Club in West Las Vegas.

I had reached a spot that would put me out in the open and I paused to survey the area. It was a long walk to the top of the hill where Harvey and Stephanie had been found. I looked at my watch and it was almost time to meet the killer. There were several excavation and grading machines to my right. I decided to go in that direction. I got down on all fours in a crouch and crawl position. As silently as I could I made my way to the back of the equipment. From my vantage point I could see the top of the hill. I checked my watch again. In twenty minutes I'd have the murderer in handcuffs.

I'd found my night goggles in my police kit and brought them along. I used them now to survey the area; they made the landscape a greenish twilight instead of near midnight. I slipped quietly to the next piece of road equipment and hid myself behind an enormous tire. I'd gone as close as I intended to the gravesite. I could see the yellow crime-scene tape even without the goggles.

I heard a faint roar behind me and knew that Ernie and his gang were on their way. They would be right on time. Within seconds, the roar became deafening and twenty Harleys screamed onto the top of the hill, circling the area. Over my right shoulder, I saw a large beam of light and heard the familiar sound of helicopter blades as they swooshed in fast rotation. I didn't need the goggles as I stood and surveyed the scene, which was lit like day from the helicopter searchlight. I knew that by now several residents would have called 911 to complain about the noise. I figured in no time several police cars would be on the scene. I was going to have to pay penance for this but it seemed to be the best way to handle the situation.

I didn't want to think about how many rules I'd broken this time. I knew the only way this episode would be in the rule book was if there was a section called: "May's Chapter – Twenty Things A Police Detective Should Never Do." As I predicted, two police cars careened onto the scene, lights flashing and tires squealing. It was one wild night on top of the mountain. The thing is, I hadn't seen anyone who looked like a killer. The patrol officers, one of which I knew, ran over to where I stood.

"Detective Scott, what's going on? Do you know anything about this? Wait a minute, is that Officer Morgan out there on that red Harley?" he asked in disbelief.

"Yes, it is, Officer Kellerman. Tell you what; I'll explain all of this in a few minutes. Right now, though, would you mind walking with me up to the gravesite?"

"Sure. Ted, why don't you go on back to the station? I can handle this one," he said to the other officer. "I'll call if anything else erupts. Detective Scott, we've had about fifty calls from the residents. What's going on? Is the noise going to go away anytime soon?" he asked very politely.

I could tell Officer Kellerman would go far with the Las Vegas Metro Police. He followed the rules and did so in a politically correct manner. Ed would have been screaming by now. Of course, Ed had to put up with me on a full-time basis, unlike Kellerman.

Before I could answer his questions, Ernie roared up on his Harley followed by his fellow club members, some of them police officers. At the same time, something that I hadn't counted on occurred. News vans from the local television stations pulled up. In a matter of minutes I had cameras and microphones thrust in my face.

"What's going on, Detective Scott?" asked Brian Stone, the most aggressive, pesky reporter in Las Vegas. He and I had disliked each other for years. How could I be so lucky to have him show up?

"You know this is a continuing crime scene, Brian. You folks shouldn't be up here. You also know this is an on going murder investigation and my comment is, 'No comment'."

"I heard you were tossed off the case, Detective Scott," another reporter asked.

They were sure the first amendment gave them rights and privileges to run roughshod over anyone who got in their way. I gazed at the young man for a moment before giving him a curt, "No comment."

Ernie came to bat for me and shooed them away. He really was a great guy, some of the time.

The helicopter hovered noisily over the crime scene. Officer Kellerman and I headed in that direction. When we reached the site it didn't take long to find what had been left for me. A steel box, like you find in a bank vault, rested directly on the site where Harvey's body was found. I pulled out latex gloves and gave a pair to Officer Kellerman. We squatted down beside the box and looked at it for a few seconds.

"Think there's a bomb in there?" he asked.

"Don't know. Think I'll just open it up," I said, full of bravado I didn't really feel.

"You really don't follow regulations do you, Detective Scott?"

"Nope." I reached for the box.

# Twelve

It didn't take long to open the box. In fact, it was so easy that I decided that's what the killer wanted. I was being played like a pawn in a chess game. There was a CD in the box, with a Dixie Chick's cover. I looked at it closer and realized it was my CD. It had been taken from my house. The killer knew enough about me to know they were my favorite singing group. This was beginning to get to me. Nobody knew that sort of stuff except Janet, Frankie, Ed, Ernie, and of course, Harvey. How in the world could this crazed person know my habits and preferences? Maybe he'd selected the CD randomly, but I doubted that. I was getting more confused by the minute.

"Detective Scott, did you hear what I said?" Officer Kellerman asked.

"No, I'm afraid I'm spacing out on you. What did you say?"

"I said we can play this CD in my patrol car. I also called in the forensics team. Do you think we should wait for them before we play it?"

"By the rules, yes, we should wait. But let's play it now. It's for me, anyway." I knew in every fiber of my being I was right.

We walked over to his patrol car and got in. Officer Kellerman handled the CD cautiously as he pushed it into the slot. The Dixie Chick's harmonious voices carried to the motorcycle riders. Ernie walked over and stood next to me as the CD continued to play.

"It's just a CD? That's weird, isn't it?" he asked.

I nodded my head in agreement. This wasn't what I'd expected.

Of course, I thought I'd have the killer in cuffs by now, and would be reading him his Miranda Rights.

I was about to say, "Let's stop it and give it to forensics," when a voice began to speak. It sounded like the person spoke through an electronic voice changer.

"Can you understand what he's saying?" Ernie asked.

The three of us leaned forward to try and pick up the garbled words coming out of the CD player.

"I know all about you, May Scott. You are the one I meant to kill. You ruined my life. I won't stop until I see you dead. I will kill everyone in your life that you care about. I'll never stop until I have you where I want you. You won't get away from me. I'm coming for you, May, and there's nowhere you can hide."

"Do you think this is a guy you put away who's back on the street now?" Ernie asked.

"It sounds like a revenge thing to me," chimed in Officer Kellerman.

"I don't know the answers to any of this. And why kill Harvey and Stephanie if I was the target?" Before we could discuss it further, the forensic team's van pulled in next to the patrol car. Three of them piled out of the van and approached the car.

I asked Ernie if he and Officer Kellerman could talk with them. I wanted to go and thank David Greer, the helicopter pilot, for doing such a great job on short notice. In all of the commotion of opening the box and listening to the CD, he had landed the chopper behind the crime scene on a flat piece of ground. I had never met him and was surprised when I walked up and saw him for the first time.

"Hi, David, I'm Detective May Scott. Thank you for helping out with this. I know you did this as a favor to Ernie, but I really appreciate your support."

"My pleasure," he said with a wonderful smile that made his eyes crinkle.

One the best looking men I've ever seen in my life reached for my offered hand and shook it. Tall, athletically slender, and darkly handsome describes him. If I lived long enough, this could get to be fun.

I gave David the information on how to bill me. It still felt strange to be giving out an attorney's name to get my bills paid. The world had certainly changed for me in the last forty-eight hours. And if the killer had his way, it was going to change for good and very soon.

I decided to listen to the CD again, that is, if I could pry it out of the hands of the forensics team. I was glad to see that Janet hadn't been called in for this one. I wanted her to stay as far away from me as possible, under the circumstances.

Unfortunately, I had no luck in getting to the CD, and who should drive up but Brenda Mitchell. When I saw her, I decided my butt had better scurry back down the mountain. Before I could get away, though, she saw me.

"May, can I talk to you for a minute?" she called, approaching at a fast gallop.

I couldn't come up with any excuses, so I simply waited for her to reach me.

"I got a call that you were chasing the murderer all over the top of the mountain. They even broke into the TV shows with a special news report. You looked really good on TV, by the way. In fact, while I was watching that, Lieutenant Frank called. I have to tell you, he's not happy about this. What's going on?"

Here was that pesky question again. What was going on? Did she really think I had any idea? So I said, "I don't have a clue."

Brenda's pleasant face took on an "I don't understand" look, which I thought nicely covered the whole incident.

"Look, Brenda, I thought I was going to catch this guy tonight, but I needed back-up. I'm not officially on this case. Actually, I'm on leave, so I couldn't go through regular channels. I asked a few favors from some friends. It just got bigger faster than I thought. All I wanted was motorcycles and a helicopter. What I got was that, plus black and whites, forensics, and TV news crews. It got out of hand. Is Lieutenant Frank really, really mad at me?"

She nodded yes. "I wish I had your moxie. I'd never have the guts to do anything like this. No wonder you have such a high profile."

"Huh? What are you talking about?" I was beginning to think I might get a letter of reprimand over this. I might have gone too far this time.

"Didn't you know the instructors at the Academy use you as an example for the new recruit classes?"

"An example of what?" I asked, not really wanting to know the answer.

"An example of a person who doesn't follow the rules, but somehow makes it turn out right anyway. You're a classic oxymoron."

Just as soon as I could find a dictionary, and someone to tell me how to spell that word, I'd look it up. I figured, though, if it had moron hooked on the end, it couldn't be that much of a compliment.

I tracked Ernie down, thanked him and his motorcycle buddies, said goodbye to the forensics crew, and headed toward my car. I figured I'd done enough damage for one night. The thing was, I still wasn't any closer to catching the killer, or even having a good idea about who it might be.

The forensics team promised to call me when they had checked the CD, not only for prints, but also for what we might not have heard due to background noise. I had the gist of it, though. I was the killer's target all along. Somehow Harvey and Stephanie had gotten in the way. At the thought of their murders, I had to stop and lean forward, bracing my hands on my knees; otherwise, I was going to pass out. All of this was too much. I wanted to find a safe place and hide away. But most of all I wanted Harvey back in my life. Tears streamed down my face and I didn't care who saw. My grief at Harvey's death came over me in waves, and though I tried hard to squelch it, this time I couldn't do it. I wanted to scream from the pain, so I did.

No one paid any attention to me, as it turned out. There was still so much activity on top of the mountain that my outburst went unnoticed. That was just as well, because now that the worst of the grief was over I wanted to drive back to the hotel, lock myself in the room, and crawl under the covers.

And that's exactly what I did.

# Thirteen

I slept until an aggravating sound woke me up. I raised my head and wondered where in the world I was as I looked around the attractive room. For a moment I thought Janet had finally convinced me to re-decorate my house and that was why it looked so updated. Then, it hit me and I knew where I was and why. I pulled the covers over my head and burrowed down in them, but the insistent ringing of the phone wouldn't stop. I threw the covers off and grabbed for the phone that sat next to the bed on a pretty little table.

"Hello," I said and yawned into the phone.

"I think I woke you up," a female voice said.

"Yes, you did. Who is this?"

"It's Anne Lambert. I was wondering if you'd like to take a drive with me today. I have some property in Pahrump. I thought it might do you good to get out of town. I saw you on television last night."

I could hear the smile in her voice. Actually, her offer sounded like a great idea.

"I'd like to go to Pahrump. It's gorgeous out there. Thank you for thinking of me."

"I've worked in law enforcement long enough that I recognize the time when you need to lay low. And you need to get out of Dodge."

I agreed to meet her in the lobby in an hour and hung up the phone. A hot shower and clean hair helped cheer me up. I couldn't do a thing about my puffy eyes. Some women look great when they cry; I'm not one of them. Oh, well, Anne would just have to take what she got.

I got to the lobby early, went into the deli and enjoyed a coffee and Danish. I could live in this place full time, although I did miss having my cat around. I'd have to call Janet and ask how Whiskers was doing. I'd left enough food and litter for twenty cats, but I'd call to make sure she was doing okay without me. Of course, cats always do fine. They don't get wrapped around the emotional axel like humans and dogs. Probably explained the nine-lives thing.

I parked myself in a comfortable wing chair positioned near the elevator that Anne would take to the lobby. As the elevator doors opened, she stepped out, right on time. I watched her progress toward me with interest. Several men in the area noticed her, too. Anne was a definite head turner.

"Good morning again," she said with a smile.

"It's certainly better than the night I had. You saw it on TV? I didn't think people in Las Vegas had time for TV, but I guess that was a wrong assumption."

"You can only enjoy the gambling for so long then you need a break. I was surprised when the news broke in showing the interview with you."

"Not nearly as surprised as I was. I wonder who tipped them off? Maybe it was one of the aggravated homeowners up there. Who knows? I don't have a clue."

"Did you learn anything about the killer?"

"No. There was a steel box with a CD in it placed where Harvey's body was found. It seems I'm the intended target. Harvey and Stephanie must have been in the wrong place at the wrong time. Forensics has the CD and box. They're putting them through their processes now. You know all about that, don't you, Anne?"

She agreed and asked, "Would you like to have breakfast before we go?"

"I had coffee and a sweet roll, but I'd be glad to sit with you while you have something. I can always go for more coffee."

We went into the deli. Anne ordered a healthy assortment of fruits and cereal.

"Do you eat healthy all the time?" I asked as I stirred my second cup of coffee with lots of cream and sugar.

"I try to. It makes me feel better."

She exuded health and beauty so whatever she was doing must work. From the top of her golden head to the bottom of her slender feet, Anne was a middle-aged goddess.

"Have you ever thought about working in Las Vegas?" I asked. "You look like you belong in this town. You fit the tall beautiful showgirl profile."

She thanked me for the compliment, but didn't answer the question.

Anne drove her rental car, which was fine with me. I was frazzled by last night's activities. I'd discovered Pahrump when I'd driven through the tiny town on my way to a mineral hot spring on the California border. No zoning laws created interesting neighborhoods and Pahrump looked like a haphazard mess to many people. But I liked the little town; there was something appealing about it. In some ways it reminded me of the small Montana farming community where I'd lived with my grandfather.

It's always amazed me how fast you can leave Las Vegas behind and get out into the desert. We hadn't gone ten miles when the look of the scenery changed dramatically. It'd been two years since I'd driven out this way and the road had doubled to four lanes. As we drove up the mountain, the terrain changed to alpine and I saw patches of snow along the side of the road. After cresting the peak we started a fast descent into the high desert valley that surrounded Pahrump.

The flat landscape was mostly shades of brown, with a few patches of green where Joshua trees and yucca grew. Signs warned motorists of the wild horses and burros that sometimes attempted to cross the highway. Several times during the year the animals were rounded up and taken to friendlier, less traveled sections of Nevada and other western states, including my home state. I developed my love of the high desert landscape when I was small and the vast plains of Eastern Montana surrounded me. Like Nevada, there were snow-capped mountain ranges in the distance. What I enjoyed about Nevada, though, was the warm weather. Montana was too cold for me, especially during the long winters.

Anne and I talked very little on the way to Pahrump. I was lost in my own thoughts of far away times in Montana and watched the brutal yet beautiful desert landscape. The sky was enormous and colored robin's egg blue. I was warm, surprisingly at peace, and thoroughly enjoying myself.

"I can't tell you how much I appreciate you suggesting this, Anne. I really needed to 'get out of Dodge'."

She smiled at me and winked.

\* \* \* \*

As we approached Pahrump, I was surprised by the growth. Anne's property was on the north side so we drove through the center of the town. The town had gained another stoplight, which brought the total up to two. There was a new casino and a shopping complex that looked like it could have been in my neighborhood in Las Vegas.

"Anne, this place has grown too much. It's getting citified. I liked it better the old way."

"Yes, it's grown. But I like having all the conveniences close by. Personally, I'm glad to see it."

As we drove out to her property, which was backed up against Bureau of Land Management acreage, the mountain views were incredible.

"This is beautiful. How did you manage to find this land?"

"I had help from a former lover of mine. He found it for me on one of his trips to the area."

She drove onto a gravel drive and stopped the car at the crest of a small hill. We got out and walked around. Mountains surrounded us. Their colors varied from gray-blue to soft purple. The closer mountains were formed of striated bands of rock that resembled ocean waves. Most were still snowcapped. A gentle breeze rustled the leaves on the cottonwoods that stood nearby; the sun warmed me to the bone. The sky had puffy white clouds; there were horses in a pasture across the road. The view was breathtaking. It was quiet, peaceful, and the air smelled fresh like spring.

"I love this place. Do you want to sell it to me?"

"No, I don't," Anne answered. "Anyway, I don't mean to be rude, but I doubt if you could afford it."

I looked at her, but didn't comment. Oh, yes, I could afford it. But then, that was my little secret.

We went to Anne's favorite restaurant for lunch. From the outside I wasn't sure I wanted to go in, because it looked like a dump. Inside, the Pasta Palace was a delight and the food was delicious. Alice, the owner, originally from New Jersey via California, had moved to Pahrump five years ago for the usual reason.

"I loved California but it was too expensive, so we moved to Nevada. We're close to the border, though, so when I really miss all those high prices, I can visit," Alice said, her New Jersey accent evident.

I couldn't resist asking, "So, if you're Alice, why didn't you name this place Alice's Restaurant?"

"I get that question all the time and here's the answer. I never go to movies, don't listen to songs, and this is the best pasta restaurant in Pahrump. It's the Pasta Palace because of that. Of course, now that I think about it, it's also the only pasta place in Pahrump," she said with a laugh.

"Makes sense to me."

There were hundreds of photos covering the walls, tables and bar. For some people, the inside of the restaurant might be claustrophobic; every space was covered with stuffed animals, lacey dolls, plates, crystal, and figurines in every size and shape. Somehow, though, it worked. It was cluttered, but in a loving grandma sort of way.

"Who're the beautiful children in the photos?" I asked.

"They're mostly my children when they were small and then my grandchildren and great grandchildren."

"You seriously can't be old enough to have great grandchildren. In fact, I'm surprised to hear you have grandkids," I said.

"I have good genes and I've had a great life. I think that sort of stuff shows on your face. But thanks, it's always nice to hear," she said.

Anne suggested I try the fettuccine with clam sauce, which was excellent.

"Are you sure you don't want to sell your property?" I asked her again.

"Yes, I'm sure, but I'll ask a real estate friend here in town to look around for something similar for you. How's that?"

"Perfect."

After lunch, we stopped by the new casino and looked around. It compared, on a much smaller scale, to the casinos in Las Vegas. Pahrump had grown and prospered at an amazing rate. Since it wasn't that far from Las Vegas, it was becoming a commuter community. I understood the pull to leave the frantic pace of Las Vegas for the serenity and slower pace that was evident in this valley.

We stopped at a grocery store before heading back to Las Vegas. I bought a couple of bottles of wine for Ernie and David Greer, the helicopter pilot.

On our way back, at dusk, Anne and I crested the peak of the mountain pass and saw the entire Las Vegas valley lit up in an amazing light display. The floor of the valley was blazing and the multicolored casino lights covered every spectrum of the rainbow. The light from the tip of the pyramid-shaped Luxor Hotel beamed into the sky like a laser. I'd heard it could be seen from as far away as Los Angeles on a clear evening.

Cars on the roads looked like strings of twinkling diamonds from this distance. Winding down from the top of the mountain pass, Las Vegas was a magical sight and one that most tourists never see. It reminded me a bit of the view that Harvey and Stephanie would've had every night, if they'd lived long enough to buy a house here.

Anne pulled into the parking lot at the back entrance of my hotel and said, "I have to go check on my flight."

"Thanks again for inviting me to go with you today. It was just what the doctor ordered. Don't fly away before I can see you again," I said, as I opened the car door and got out.

"Oh, don't worry, we'll see each other again," she said with a wave as she pulled away from the curb.

I turned and walked toward the hotel. I knew I'd have several messages waiting for me when I got to my room and I was right. Most of them were from Lieutenant Frank and Ed. Both of them were furious and they had a right to be.

# Fourteen

Later I agonized over my decision to turn my phone off, after listening to several blistering messages, and go to bed. At the time it seemed like a good idea. I began to understand what the lieutenant and Ed had meant when they told me I was too close to the case. I couldn't seem to sort out facts that made any sense. All I wanted to do was burrow under the covers and hide. Part of it was that I was scared. There was, after all, a killer on my trail. Somehow I had enraged this person enough to kill Harvey and Stephanie. The only time I was able to close out the horror was when I slept. My dreams weren't filled with anything that scared me, which was strange under the circumstances. But I took advantage of it and slept soundly.

A pounding on the door woke me up. I came out from under the covers and stumbled to the door. "Who is it?"

"It's me, Ed. Are you all right?"

I took the chain off the door, unbolted both locks, and removed the chair I'd propped under the handle. I opened the door, looked at Ed's surprised face, and only then realized I had on my nightgown.

"Oops!" I said, slamming the door in his face. I grabbed my robe from the bathroom, put it on and re-opened the door.

"I'm sorry. I didn't mean to horrify you like that. Why do you still look so upset? Is something wrong, other than the fact that you just saw me in my nightgown?"

"Mrs. Bride has been murdered."

Cold chills covered my body and black spots danced before my eyes. I grabbed at the door to keep myself upright. "What? That sweet little lady who stays in the hotel? Why would someone kill her? When did it happen? How did she die?"

"The maid found her this morning when she went in to clean the room. She was shot, just like Harvey and Stephanie. Janet is down there now and she said it looks to her like a mirror image of Stephanie's murder. Remember how she was positioned? That's the way Mrs. Bride's body looks, too. Has anybody been to your room? Have you been contacted in any way? Any strange messages on your phone?"

"No, nothing. I came in fairly early, around eight, listened to you and the Lieutenant scream at me. Janet called to say all was well with her and Frankie and that Whiskers was doing good. Rick left a couple of messages, too, but that was to remind me for the thousandth time that I need to fly to Tacoma and check out the box Harvey left for me at the bank. Other than that, nothing." I walked over to the bed and sat down.

Ed came into the room and closed the door firmly behind him. "We have to get you out of here. You know that, don't you, May? He's getting too close to you. Do you have any idea why he'd go after Mrs. Bride, of all people?"

"I have no idea. She was just a harmless older woman who looked lonely. She lived in this hotel most of the time, but she also stayed in others around Las Vegas. She didn't have much information about Harvey and Stephanie other than the fact that she rode down in the elevator with them. Did Brenda find out anything when she re-interviewed her?"

"Nothing more than what you just said."

Ed and I looked at each other and I knew we were thinking the same thing. The killer had been very close to me, only a few floors away, and knew I'd interviewed Mrs. Bride. How long did I have until he found me and explained what I had done to ruin his life? Of course, I might never find out if he killed me first without an explanation. I started shaking and the black spots returned.

When I woke up, I was back in the hospital in the same room I'd had after the attack a few days earlier. I looked around at the familiar white walls as tears streamed down my face. All I had to keep me company was the thought that I was a wealthy woman. Somehow, that didn't matter at all, because the price was much too high.

"Aunt May? Can you hear me? I have a visitor here to see you."

I was swimming up from the depths of a watery grave. The voice brought me to the surface and I knew Frankie was with me. I opened my eyes and saw his blurry form. There was another blurry form that looked like some sort of black and white squiggly animal. Then I realized it was Whiskers.

"Whiskers?" I asked, as I reached out for my fat, furry cat. "How did you get her into the hospital?"

Frankie smiled. "I've spent most of my life between here and the morgue. I know all the secret ways to get in."

"You know, I'm beginning to think your mother and I did you a disservice by letting you follow us around as much as we did."

"No, it's cool. That's why I've known since I was ten years old that I was going to be a doctor. Whiskers is a great cat, isn't she?"

"Yes, she saved my life, if you remember." I petted her and she lay on top of my stomach and purred.

"This is the best gift you could have brought me; a visit from the two of you. Just what the doctor ordered."

"Mom said you were upset over the old lady's death. That it put you back in the hospital. You've been taking the meds they gave you, haven't you, Aunt May?"

"You sound like a doctor, Frankie. You'll make a great one. Just remember some day in the future when something gets sneaked into a room, that it really can help the patient, even if it's not authorized."

We spent a few more minutes chatting until my doctor came in, followed by a nurse.

"Well, May, I see you have visitors. I know Frankie, but who's the fuzzy one on your tummy?" Dr. Wells asked, as he petted the purring cat.

"This is Whiskers. She saved my life."

"Ah, the cat that meowed until you woke up after being attacked. I read about it in the paper."

"That was in the paper?" Why didn't I know that?

82

"On TV, too," the nurse commented, as she straightened the covers on my bed.

"You seem to get a lot of press coverage, I've noticed," Dr. Wells said, with a grin. "Could it be because you're always in some sort of hot water?"

"Beats me."

"I tell you what, Frankie, it's okay that you brought Whiskers in this time, but please don't do it again. Germs, you know."

"Gotcha, Doc. I'll take her back to my dad's house. He's here visiting one of his troops, so I came along. Mom, Whiskers, and I are staying with him for a while. I think it has something to do with Aunt May's problem."

All four of them looked at me. I shook my head in wonder. How could such a skinny, little redhead like me get into so many jams?

I felt much better after Frankie and Whisker's visit, but I wanted to get back to the murder investigation. I got off the bed, intending to find my purse and cell phone. I didn't get far before the room starting spinning. I clutched the edge of the bed and held on until it stopped.

"Are you trying to hold the bed down, May?" Rick asked, a perplexed look on his face, as he walked into the room.

The vertigo subsided and I let go of the bed. "No, I'm trying not to fall on the floor. It was just a dizzy spell."

Rick looked splendid. He was an attractive guy and he smelled wonderful. "You're a sight for sore eyes," I said, as I looked him up and down.

"You, too," he responded. "I don't think I've ever had a client who gets in as much trouble as you, May."

"I just had that discussion. Let's talk about something else. What is that aftershave you have on? I love the way you smell."

"I don't have on any aftershave."

"Then why do you always smell so good to me?"

"Because you and I are attracted to each other. Haven't you figured that out by now?"

He leaned in to kiss me, but I pulled back. "I must be a mess and

I haven't brushed my teeth, and…"

He just kept coming and kissed me anyway. I didn't see stars or hear music, but I definitely liked it.

"I've wanted to do that since the first time you walked into my office. In fact, I've had to restrain myself every time I'm around you."

We were about to really kiss when I heard a loud knock.

"You must be feeling better," Ed growled, clearly annoyed at finding me in Rick's arms.

Why is it I have such problems with romance? "Couldn't you have called, Ed?"

"No, I couldn't have called. I need to talk to you in private," he said, pointedly looking at Rick.

"I have to go anyway. We'll start again where we left off." He gave me a quick brush with his lips on my cheek. I sighed with happiness.

Rick left and Ed stepped up next to the bed. "You just won't listen to me, will you?"

"About what?" I feigned ignorance.

"I've told you I don't trust that guy. I come in here, to your hospital bed, and he's all over you."

"He wasn't all over me. Anyway, have you found out anything bad about him?"

"Not yet, but you'll be the first to know when I do," he assured me.

"How're the investigations coming along?"

"Brenda is checking Mrs. Bride's background. It appears she wasn't exactly an angel."

"What in the world are you talking about?"

"She was a player. A shark. The hotels knew it and watched her like a hawk. They figured it was better to know where she was than to just let her roam around loose."

"You're kidding. That little old lady conned the casinos?"

"No, they knew what she was about, they just watched her. They didn't want her fleecing the guests. That's bad for their business and image. She was a clever con artist, according to hotel security."

"And I thought she was a lonely old lady lost and alone in the world."

"You didn't get a clue when you saw she was living in a casino hotel? That might have been a big tip, May. Sometimes I wonder about your reasoning. Frankly, it sucks."

"You're just mad at me because of Rick. Why don't you want me to be happy?"

"I do want you to be happy. That's why I'm having a background check done on him. There is one thing I know about him. He's married."

My rosy dream world began to disintegrate. "Married?"

"Big time. He's married to a very wealthy woman and they have three kids."

"Three kids?"

"Will you stop repeating everything I say to you? What type of meds are you on? You seem to be dingier than usual."

"Why didn't he tell me?"

"Did you ever ask?"

He had me there. "No, I never asked."

"You probably knew it, but wouldn't admit it. Anyway, that makes him perfect for you, doesn't it, May? He's unavailable, unreliable, and a liar. Just the way you like them. Guaranteed to make you miserable and break your heart. I can't figure why you're hanging around with a lawyer anyway. You don't even like lawyers."

My back was to Ed so he didn't see my face, which I'm sure looked guilty. I needed to tell him about the will.

"I don't want you to get hurt like you did with Ernie."

"I'm over Ernie."

"Sure you are. You found his replacement with Rick. And it's like I told you, he's even worse than Ernie. Ernie is stupid. Rick isn't. He's a clever dirt bag, which makes him more dangerous for you than Ernie."

I crawled into bed and pulled the covers over my head. "Just go away, Ed. I don't want to hear anymore." I heard him leave and I was glad. I'd explain it to him some other time. All I wanted to do was sleep.

# Fifteen

I've never understood how you're supposed to rest in a hospital because they never leave you alone. Every time I tried to go back to sleep, someone would wake me up for another test, a walk, or a consultation. I was exhausted and irritated. When Dr. Wells showed up again, I asked him when I could leave.

"Just as soon as we have one more test, get it evaluated, and then I can give you an answer."

"You aren't going to tell me, are you?"

"Yes, when we know what we're dealing with."

"I thought the hit on my head was the problem."

"Yes, that caused the initial problem. But we have to find out why you keep blacking out, May. That could come from any number of causes and we need to isolate the particular reason."

"Is that officer still outside my door?"

"Yes, he is."

"Could it be you're keeping me here because it's a safe place for me to stay? Did Ed and Lieutenant Frank set this up?"

"We don't have room or time to be guards, May. No, you're here because you're ill and we're trying, as fast as we can, to find the cause of your black outs."

"I haven't had one in a little while now. That's good, isn't it?"

"Yes, that is good. But, we don't want you to have any at all, May. Black outs can be very serious. You know that. We've talked about it."

"I know. I'm just so sick of being sick. I'm not used to it."

"Believe me, we won't keep you in here any longer than necessary. We're only trying to help you."

"I know. I just don't like being in here."

He smiled, said, "Rest now," patted my hand and left.

* * * *

When I woke, it was dark. The room was in shadows and the door was closed. I slowly edged off the bed and carefully crossed the room to go to the bathroom. I turned the bathroom light on and took a good look at myself. Grief, what a mess! I'd decided to take a shower when I heard the room door opening very slowly. Quickly, I cut off the light in the bathroom and nudged the door almost closed. I peeped through the slight opening and watched as a tall, slender figure entered my room. He was dressed in dark clothes, head to toe, and had some sort of covering over his face. I knew it was the murderer. My gun was gone because Ed had taken it away from me. The figure moved toward the bed and in the gloom I knew he couldn't tell that the mound under the covers wasn't me, but my pillows. I watched as he pulled a small gun from his jacket and shot twice. The silencer worked so well that all I heard was a muffled crack. I waited for him to pose the body, but he didn't. He left the room, closing the door quietly behind him.

I came out from the bathroom, and started to open the door when I realized, even though he had on gloves, forensics might come up with something on the knob. I grabbed a towel from the bathroom and gingerly opened the door, trying to make as little contact as possible with the metal. The long hall was empty. The officer who had been stationed outside my door was absent and the murderer had disappeared. I went to the phone and called Ed, waking him from a sound sleep.

"Detective Daniels speaking," he answered groggily.

"Ed, he tried to kill me again tonight. But he killed the bed pillows instead."

"Are you all right? Where was the officer who was supposed to be outside your door?"

"I don't know, and yes, I'm all right."

"I'm on my way. Lock the door and don't open it for anyone but me."

I did exactly as Ed told me to do. Now, that was a first.

\* \* \* \*

It didn't take long for the usual crew to show up. In fact, it was getting a little old, this convening of police, forensics, and news crews. How the reporters found out about it, I didn't know. The sad part was, if the information about the pillows being shot instead of me hadn't been reported so fast, it would have been a plus for the murder investigation. Now the killer knew I was still alive.

"Tell me again," Ed asked. "What made you get up at just that time?"

"I woke up and had to go to the bathroom. I don't know why I woke up at that exact moment. Maybe my guardian angels were watching out for me."

"Somebody was watching out for you, all right. What can you tell me about the killer? Let's go over this one more time."

I repeated it over and over again for Ed, Brenda, and even Lieutenant Frank when he showed up. Rick appeared on the scene and managed to talk his way into the room.

"How did you get past the gauntlet?" I asked.

"It's a talent I have. It's what got me into law to start with, my 'gift of gab'."

"If you have this great gift, why didn't you gab to me that you're married and have three children?"

He was silent, but did have the good grace to look guilty.

"Where's the gab, Rick?"

"Let me explain," he said.

As soon as it was out of his mouth I knew Ed had been right about him.

"That's okay, you've explained yourself perfectly. Still, I do need an attorney and since Ed hasn't found anything negative about your law practice you can do that for me. And how did you find out about this so fast? You seem to have an amazing ability to show up just at the right time."

Rick looked shamefaced. "I was coming to see you anyway; then I ran into a reporter I know down in the lobby and she told me."

Brenda came up and asked if I could talk with her and part of the forensics team, which was a blessing. I did want to get away from Rick. I saw Ed watching me from across the room and nodded to him. He nodded back, so he knew I understood what he'd told me about Rick was true.

Brenda did a good job and I was impressed. As I talked with her, I saw a visibly agitated officer run into my small hospital room and whisper into Lieutenant Frank's ear. He followed the officer out of the room while we watched. Ed motioned for me to follow but then I realized it was Brenda he wanted, not me. I felt like a wallflower.

I sat down on the edge of the bed and tried to make sense of the past few days. I couldn't do it. It made no sense. Rick came over and tried to talk to me, but I didn't want anything to do with him. My attitude had changed one hundred and eighty degrees in the last hour. He insisted that I listen to him, though, so I did.

"Okay, I'm a rat. I'm not faithful to my wife. I'm attracted to you and I'm sorry if I was out of bounds. However, I am a damn good lawyer and you need me," he said. "Your life has changed in ways you don't even know about yet, so whether you dislike me or not, we're going to be a team, at least in business. Until you fire me, I have a signed contract to provide legal services for you and I will do that. And call Ed off. There's nothing to find on me as far as my law firm is concerned. I'm A+ in that department."

"I never told him to check you out. He did it on his own because he distrusted you on sight. I'm glad to hear you're such a great lawyer, because you're right, I do need one. So until you screw that up, I won't fire you."

Ed came back into the room and said, "Every person who isn't law enforcement or medical, leave now." Since the only person who didn't fall into one of those categories was Rick, it was clear he had to leave. He left and didn't look back.

"Listen up, please. The body of the officer who was on duty outside May's door was found. We'll need to take statements from all medical personnel who were on duty during the past four hours. Detective Brenda Mitchell is outside in the hall and she'll talk with each of you. Thanks in advance for your cooperation and patience."

I was stunned. This brought the number of bodies to four. The young officer was still in probation period. Why in the world had he been killed? Before I could ask that question, Ed came up and explained.

"Officer Lomas must have seen the guy leave, followed him, and was shot in the head, just like the other three victims. It looks like Lomas tore off a piece of the black jacket the killer was wearing, probably the pocket. It's still clutched in his hand, so at least we have something to go on. He called the station to say he was going to the bathroom, and when he got back, he must have seen the killer leaving your room. He called the station again and asked for back up and for you to be checked on by the medical staff. Officer Lomas, though young, did everything by the book, but it didn't help him. We're also checking the cameras to see if anything got caught on film. So far it looks as if the killer managed to stay out of range of the cameras. We're still working on that part of it. One thing is certain. We aren't dealing with a dumb one. This is a smart guy who knows how to cover all the angles. Makes me wonder if he's one of us."

"No, that makes no sense at all. I think it must be tangled up in the will. Some mad relative feels he got cheated out of Harvey's money."

"What are you talking about? What money? What will?"

I knew I should've disclosed this information as soon as I knew about it.

"Harvey made me his sole heir."

Ed looked at me in disbelief. "He did what?"

"Harvey made me a very rich woman. I should have told you and Brenda as soon as I found out. I'm sorry."

"This changes the whole tenor of the case. What's wrong with you? Why didn't you tell me this?"

I could tell Ed was at the end of his rope with me and I didn't blame him.

"Look, all I've done is screw up. Every choice I've made has been bad and what I think is black is white. I guess I'm in such turmoil over Harvey and Stephanie's death, Mrs. Bride, plus this young officer that I'm just not thinking straight."

"That explains why Rick is always hanging around. I tell you, I still think he's involved in this somehow. How did he get to be your lawyer?"

"The Tacoma lawyers that Harvey had used for years called on Rick to handle the will for them in Las Vegas. I think Rick is on the up and up as far as his law practice, Ed, but you were right on target about his family. He's a rat. Thank you for setting me straight."

"Somebody has to. You don't have enough sense to get out of bed in the morning." He smiled when he said it, so I knew we were okay again.

"Now, Miss Money Bags, sit down on that bed and tell me all about this fortune you have instead of someone in Harvey's family."

# Sixteen

Ed and I talked for about an hour, with constant interruptions from Brenda or the medical staff, who seemed to think I was still in need of their attention. All of it was getting old fast.

"Ed, I need to get out of here. I'm well enough to leave. Let me get out of this hospital gown and into my clothes and we can leave."

"Whoa, there. I don't think you're ready for that. You do need to be moved to another hospital, though."

He got up to talk with Brenda, who was still in the hall, about moving me, when the telephone next to my bed rang.

"Hello."

"So, I shot the pillows instead of you? Well, don't think that little miss will stop me. You'll be deader than all the rest of them very soon. And you'll be sorry for what you did to me."

The phone went dead and I knew he'd hung up. It was the same sort of disguised, electronic voice I'd heard twice before. I sighed as I sat on the bed and continued to hold the receiver in my hand. That's how Ed found me when he came back into the room.

"What happened? Who was on the phone?"

"The killer. He told me I'd be sorrier than all of them when I was dead, because of what I've done to him. What have I done to him, Ed? I don't know."

"You haven't done anything wrong, May. He's crazy. And you're so drugged up you look half dead. Get under the covers and go to sleep. Didn't they just give you something to make you sleep? We'll get you moved to another hospital in the morning. Are you okay?

Your eyes look like they're glazed over."

I tried to speak, but I felt myself falling down the rabbit hole again. Soon, all of this would go away and I would be at peace.

\* \* \* \*

When I woke up again the room was dark and empty. I guess the party had ended. I sat up and looked at the clock on the little table next to the bed. It was early evening. I swung my legs over the side and tentatively put my feet onto the cold, tiled floor. I stood then walked slowly into the bathroom. I stopped for a moment, as I had a strange sense of déjà vu. I waited for a moment, to see if the killer would re-enter my room and try to shoot me all over again. I shook my head to clear it, went into the bathroom, and splashed cold water on my face. That woke me up. I found my slippers, put them on my cold feet, slipped on my robe and went to the door. I cautiously pulled it open and peeped out. The sight of the uniformed officer comforted me. I opened the door wider and stepped out.

"Thank you for standing watch," I said to him. I noticed he was much older than the previous officer.

"My pleasure, Detective Scott. Is there anything you need?" he asked.

"No, I just wanted to make sure I thanked you. I didn't get a chance to tell Officer Lomas that before he was killed. Please, please be careful and don't let anything happen to you."

"I'll make every effort to keep us both alive."

He said it with such intensity that all I could do was believe him. I closed my door, went back to bed and didn't wake up until the nurse came in to give me another injection to help me sleep.

I decided I'd had enough of the hospital when I woke up. I got up, showered, put my clothes on and proceeded to the nurse station.

"I wanted to thank all of you," I said to the nurses who were there. "I'm checking myself out now; what do I need to do?" I asked in all innocence, thinking this would be a simple process. About two hours later, after having been lectured by half the hospital staff and terrorized by the lady who handled billing and insurance, I walked through the huge front doors of the hospital, vowing never to return. You have to be a hospital person to like these places and I definitely wasn't one of those.

Of course, where I was going wouldn't be a choice hangout for most people. I needed to talk with Dr. Williams, at the morgue, about the young officer who had died protecting me. I still couldn't make sense of the fact that a strong, well-trained young man could have been so neatly shot through the head with no evidence of a struggle, except the piece of pocket he had torn off the killer's jacket. Something wasn't adding up and I figured Dr. Williams would have the answer.

I took one of the many cabs that waited outside the hospital entrance. Unless it had been moved, my car would be at Caesar's Palace. Ed hadn't said anything about it so I hoped it was still there. The cabbie let me out in the underground garage and I saw that my car was where I'd parked it. I paid him, walked up to my car, unlocked it and got in.

I drove down the congested streets to the morgue. It was amazing how fast the valley had grown and changed in just the few years that I'd lived in Las Vegas. Maps couldn't be printed fast enough to keep up with the new streets and subdivisions that were being built all over town. I pulled into the parking lot, got out of my car and walked into the building. Maybe it was my imagination but this building felt colder than any of the others that I went into on a regular basis. I'd asked Janet about that once and she'd laughed at me. "That's your overheated imagination," she'd said. "It's not colder than any of the other buildings." Perhaps, but it didn't seem that way to me. I punched in the code to open the unmarked elevator doors. I certainly didn't want to be back this soon, because I've never liked morgues, but here I was again, walking toward the large double doors. After entering the code on the keypad I pushed the right door open and entered. I didn't see Dr. Williams in the office area, so I walked toward the examination room where I knew I'd find him. Sure enough he was there with his assistant. The large, white room was spotlessly clean and scary.

"Hello, Dr. Williams. Hello Molly." They were so intent on their work that they didn't look up.

"I heard you were back in the hospital. What're you doing here?" Dr. Williams asked, as he continued to pull out body organs so Molly could weight them.

"I wanted to talk to you about Officer Lomas, the young officer who was murdered at the hospital. When are you posting him?"

"I already have. Molly and I started early today."

Molly, a student from the University of Utah Medical College, was interning with him. I thought of Frankie and realized that someday he would be rotating through a morgue, maybe this one, during his training to become a doctor. Molly had decided that her niche was in the morgue. She couldn't have found a better mentor than Dr. Williams.

"What did you find out?"

"It was a clean shot to the head, but some sort of stun gun was used on him first."

"That's what I couldn't figure out. I knew there had to be more to it than I've been told. Did you find anything like that on Harvey, Stephanie, or Mrs. Bride?"

"Yes, I did."

"Why didn't I know that? I was with you when you posted Harvey and Stephanie and I don't remember anything about a stun gun." I was getting upset.

"If you will recall, May, you passed out and spent most of that visit on the couch in my office. I didn't finish with the victims until later, after you'd already been told by Lieutenant Frank to go on vacation. So, you weren't privy to details like that."

"Oh, you think so? Well, who do you think this guy is really after? Me! I should have been told he was using a stun gun. It could save my life to know that."

"You've got a point, May. Talk to Ed and Brenda about it. They know everything."

"What type of stun gun was it? Could you tell?"

"It was heavy duty because it disabled a big guy like the officer.

All it took was to apply pressure once and he was down. In Lomas's case, it was used on his chest. His shirt was thin, so his clothing didn't do much to protect him. If he'd had on his protective vest with the ceramic inserts, it might have saved him, or at least given him more of a chance to fight back."

"You don't think the killer used a taser? That thing would bring down an elephant."

"The marks look like a stun gun, about 3.5 centimeters apart and resemble a burn on the skin. The taser makes marks that look more like a bee sting and are hard, if not impossible, to detect."

"Thanks for talking with me and I'm not angry. I'm just upset about everything, I guess."

"You've got a right to be, May. Take care of yourself and do what everybody has advised. Go on holiday for a few days. It might be the smartest thing in this situation. Let Ed and Brenda catch this guy."

I said my goodbyes and left the morgue. At least I'd been right about one thing. Officer Lomas didn't have much of a chance after he'd been stunned. It doesn't matter how athletic or strong you are; when one of those weapons comes in contact with a body, you're going down.

After I started back to my car, it dawned on me I didn't have anywhere to go. My house still had crime tape around it. The hotel was out and now so was the hospital. Everywhere I went, the killer followed.

When I walked outside, I smelled the wonderful aroma of the Seattle coffee shops that seem to be on every corner. I went in and got a blueberry scone and latte. I purposely picked the most distant table from the entrance and sat where I could watch as people came through the line. Although I was still a part of the Las Vegas Metro Police, I felt like an outsider. As Dr. Williams had pointed out I was no longer in the loop. I wasn't sure where I belonged. My life had changed so completely over the past few days, it overwhelmed and frightened me.

* * * *

After I ate I walked back to my little car. It felt good to be behind the wheel again. The hospital staff had cautioned me about driving, but I chose to ignore their warning. I decided to go back to the hotel to reclaim my few belongings. Ed had left a message on my cell phone telling me the hotel staff had packed my bag and stored it near the registration desk. I pulled into the front of the hotel and let the valet park my car. I went to the registration counter in the lobby, retrieved my suitcase and settled the account. I was back in the car and on my way within fifteen minutes. I thought I should suggest to the hospital that they make it as easy to check out of their facility.

I was driving aimlessly down the Strip when I saw David Greer's sign advertising helicopter tours. On a whim, I pulled into a parking space in front of the building and saw him through the window. I opened my suitcase, rummaged around, and found the bottle of wine I had bought for him in Pahrump. Using the small mirror in my handbag, I applied lipstick and combed my short hair with my fingers.

As I walked toward the door, I saw that David had his eyes glued to a computer screen. I pushed open the door and a bell tinkled.

"Does that mean an angel just got her wings?" I asked with a smile.

"It looks like an angel just walked in the door. I was hoping I'd see you again, May Scott."

"I got this for you when I went to Pahrump the other day. I hope you like wine."

"I love wine. When can we drink it together?"

"Anytime you want."

"Let's go," he said. He went to the door, turned the Open sign to Closed, asked if I had locked my car, then locked the door, and turned out the lights.

"Let me turn off the computer and I'm ready," he said.

I followed him out the back of the building and toward a long blue truck. "Where are we going?" I belatedly asked.

"Let's go out to Red Rock Canyon. We can polish off this bottle and get to know each other," he said.

After the last few days, the time I spent with David was a gift. Of course, up front I asked, "Are you married, engaged, going steady, somehow tied up with a woman, or gay?"

He laughed and said, "Nope. I'm divorced, have no kids, no girlfriends, and I'm most definitely not gay, which I hope someday soon to prove to you."

"Sounds promising. Ernie told me you're in the Air Force Reserve."

"After I got off active duty, I went Reserve. When I'm not flying tourists all over the southwest, I work at Indian Springs Air Force Base, not far from where my house is located. You'll have to come out and visit. Mt. Charleston is practically in my back yard. It's peaceful and beautiful out there."

My, my, my… you just never know what's around the next bend.

# Seventeen

"Hello, Ed? Are you awake?"

"What time is it, May? Where are you? I called every hospital in the area looking for you yesterday. And now I'm awake."

"Do you know David Greer? He's Ernie's friend, the helicopter pilot? He helped me out the other night when I hired him to fly over the murder scene."

"No, I don't know him, but if he's a friend of Ernie's, he's no good."

"Will you stop that? I'm getting sick and tired of your judgmental attitude. Who made you king?"

"I'm going on past behavior and common sense, which you don't have."

"Do, too!"

"Do not!"

"We sound like we're about ten years old, Ed."

"Yeah, well, that's how you act."

"I called to tell you I've moved in with David Greer."

Silence.

"What did you say?"

"I've moved in with David Greer, Ernie's friend."

"Why?"

"Because I didn't have anywhere else to go and he asked me."

"Why did he ask you?"

"Because he likes me. He thinks I'm cute."

"You're not cute. You're a pain in the butt. He just doesn't know that yet."

"It'll be temporary, until I can figure what else to do. He's a terrific guy, Ed."

"Uh, huh."

"No, he is. This time it's different. And yes, I asked if he had a wife, or any other sort of woman in his life, and he doesn't. He's not gay, either."

"Uh, huh."

"Will you stop saying that?"

"Huh, uh."

"You treat me like I don't have good sense."

More silence.

"Hello? Are you there?"

"Uh, huh."

"Ed, you're acting like a woman who's had her feelings hurt. Why do you get so upset over the men in my life?"

"Because I hate to see you getting used by all these dirt bags you pick out."

"Honest, Ed, this guy is different."

"Uh, huh."

"Do you want his number and address or not?"

"Let me have it. And don't come whining to me when he turns out to be a jerk."

"He's not a jerk. He's got a nice, little house out toward Indian Springs on the road to Mount Charleston. We talked all night and I told him everything about what's going on. He offered to let me stay at his place. It's sort of remote out here and off the beaten track. I like it. The sky is beautiful and there's no traffic noise. Not that it's any of your business, but we haven't had sex yet, though it's on my mind."

"I don't need to know anything but the address and phone number."

"Well, you're always so nosy about my male friends. If I didn't know better, I'd think you were jealous."

"I'm not jealous. Just concerned, because you have no brains when it comes to your boyfriends."

"He's not a boyfriend. Yet."

After hanging up, I walked outside and looked around. David's house was one-half mile off the main road. I was out here with the sky, horses, mountains and sunshine. It reminded me of Anne's property in Pahrump, with the snow-capped mountains close by. David had left for work early as he had a full day of flying tourists over Las Vegas, plus trips out to Hoover Dam and the Grand Canyon. I didn't expect to see him until late in the evening, which was fine with me.

He was an interesting man and I hoped we could develop a relationship that meant something; however, it was too soon to tell. I decided I should let Rick and Janet know where I was so I called. Both of them were in. I made an appointment to meet with Rick at his office that afternoon.

Janet agreed with Dr. Williams that a stun gun had been used on all the victims. "I want you to promise me that you'll wear your vest everywhere you go."

"I have it in the back of my car and I'll wear it, I promise. How's Frankie coming along with his sweetie?"

"What sweetie? I don't know anything about any 'sweetie'."

"I guess I shouldn't have said anything. He has a crush on a girl in his class. Her name is Kim."

"I have no idea about that. Maybe his dad knows something about it. I'll ask him."

"Are you enjoying your stay with Tom? It seems this has disrupted lots of lives since Harvey and Stephanie were murdered, not just mine."

"Murder always disrupts lives. And yes, we're doing fine. I like living on the base. Everything is so convenient," Janet said.

"Does that mean you two will finally get back together?"

"We've never really been apart, just led separate lives. My career was, in some ways, more demanding than his."

"I know that. I lived through a big chunk of it with you."

"Yeah, you're right. What can I say? I have a strange marriage. Sometimes I feel more single than married, but I know in my heart he's the only man I'll ever love. And that's how he feels about me, too."

"It sounds wonderful to me, but then, I'm the original 'do it wrong girl,' when it comes to men."

"Don't I know that. How many times have we talked about your bad habits, girl? Who's this David guy? Ernie's friend? That can't be good, May."

"You're beginning to sound more and more like Ed. Do you know that?"

"We've discussed you, too, and we agree you're clueless when it comes to guys. The only thing you get right is they're all too handsome for their own good."

"Well, looks are important, don't you think?"

"Not if it replaces love, honesty, and commitment."

"I get the picture. So, you know where I am, you're all okay, and Whiskers owns your heart. Right?"

"Right. Be careful and wear that vest with the ceramic inserts."

"I promise."

\* \* \* \*

I went into the house, showered and washed my hair, which always improves my mood, then made a pot of coffee. I felt right at home in David's house. I wandered around, coffee cup in hand and looked at his few possessions. He had a couple of photos out and I looked at them. From the resemblance, they must be his family members. What a handsome group, tall and dark. I guessed it was mom, dad, and sister. The other photo was of a little girl, but I had no idea who she might be. I'd have to ask him sometime soon. After being burned so often by men and the constant warnings from Ed and Janet, and Harvey before them, I was beginning to question my feelings and actions. Maybe what Harvey had tried to tell me over the years had finally sunk into my skull. It still seemed unreal to me that he was gone. I hoped he would contact me after death. He could reassure me that he and Stephanie were alive, well and happy in another existence. So far, though, all I had were dead bodies piling up because of our relationship.

I looked at the clock and realized I needed to get on the road to make my appointment with Rick. I dreaded seeing him. I felt I had made a fool of myself over him and now, here I was, linked to him because of all that money. Poor, sad, filthy rich little me.

The drive didn't take long because I was on the right side of town. I pulled into the parking area in front of the impressive, new building that housed Rick's offices and parked next to a familiar looking car. I shut off the engine, got out, looked at the car for a moment and realized it was exactly like Anne Lambert's rental. I peeped inside, but it was empty. I walked around the car and noted that it had a Nevada tag. For some reason, I pulled out my notebook and wrote the number down. "Get a grip," I told myself, as I walked toward the large, double-glass doors, but I put the number in my purse.

This time, I knew where I was going and why. The first time I visited Rick, my entire life changed. I didn't have to wait and went back to his large, corner office.

"Hello, May, it's good to see you. We really need to talk."

"Here I am."

"When are you going to Tacoma?"

"I thought I'd go in a couple of days."

"Albert Catrel, Harvey's primary lawyer, has called me daily asking when you'll arrive."

"I know. I need to get this show on the road, don't I?"

"Yes."

"Can't one of those high-priced lawyers up there open up the box and tell me what's inside?"

"No, May. That's not how it works"

"Well, it should."

"Do you want me to fly up there with you? I could make all the arrangements for us."

I paused. Less than a week ago I would have been ecstatically happy at the thought of spending time with Rick.

"No, I'll go alone."

"You hate me now, don't you?"

"No, I don't hate you. I just don't want to have anything to do with you in any way, but business."

"This is business. I'm your attorney. I should be there with you."

"Do you know how much that would cost me? Do you think I'm made out of money?"

"I know every penny you have, plus I can project how much more will be coming in daily. You can afford me. And more importantly, you need me."

I sighed, paused, and agreed. He had a point. I didn't know anything about this sort of thing and he was my attorney. "Only business, no dinners, no drinks, no nothing. Understand?"

"That's fine with me."

"Do you know Anne Lambert?"

"No, who is she?"

"She's the Medical Examiner from Reno. She was here for the same conference as Harvey. I thought I saw her rental in the parking lot."

"All rental cars look alike, you know that."

"Yeah, I guess you're right. A good-looking, tall blond doesn't ring any bells?"

"Only good-looking redheads ring my bell."

"Cut that out! You promised!"

"Sorry. I forgot. By the way, would you like to hear about my marriage?"

"No."

"Okay, but it's not how you think it is."

"I want no details. You're my lawyer and that's all."

"I'll get our trip set up and call you with the information."

"And don't make it first class. I'm not paying for you to fly fancy."

"Yes, ma'am, got it. We'll fly business class. That's a happy medium."

I spent a few more minutes with him and then went back to my car. I noticed the car that looked like Anne's was gone. Rick was right. All rentals look alike.

# Eighteen

Since I was close to the freeway and it wasn't a heavy commute time, I decided to go into the office. It wasn't congested on the roads, so I got to the station in about fifteen minutes. It dawned on me that I was using commute times to determine how to get around Las Vegas. It reminded me of what I used to do in Tacoma and Seattle. Since that was one of the reasons I left the Northwest for dry, sunny Nevada with its empty roads, an alarm bell went off in my head. I wondered if my time in Las Vegas was about over.

I don't like to sit in backed up traffic; maybe that was because I was raised in the wide-open ranges of Eastern Montana. It made me fondly recall my trip with Anne out to small, non-congested Pahrump. I really would have to pursue buying property out there. Considering what had gone on, for the past couple of weeks, this was positive thinking. I enjoyed thoughts of living in Pahrump surrounded by peace, quiet, and snowcapped mountains. If I got bored, Las Vegas would be less than an hour away.

With any luck, Lieutenant Frank would be out of the office, and Ed and Brenda would be in. Lucky for me that's what occurred. I spent about an hour talking to Ed and my new friend Brenda.

"Why didn't one of you tell me about the stun gun used on the victims? I talked to Dr. Williams and he said that you've known since day one. Why was I left out of the loop on this, when I'm the target?"

"We talked about that, but you were in the hospital, twice. Brenda and I thought that we could protect you better if you didn't know everything that was going on. I know you, May," Ed said. "You would worry yourself into a frenzy, trying to figure out what the killer would do next. I talked to your doctors and they advised against telling you, so that's what we did."

"We truly thought it was in your best interest," Brenda said. "And we still believe it was the correct decision."

"Should I be wearing any sort of protection? Janet told me I should be in my vest all the time, so I have it on right now. Is that going to do any good, do you think? Or am I a walking dead woman?"

Ed sighed. I could tell he was wrestling with whatever it was that he didn't want to tell me. "I wish we could answer that. So far, we haven't got any clear leads. We're in contact with relatives of all four of the victims, especially Harvey and Stephanie. In fact, they're pitching fits to have the bodies released so they can have burial services."

"What we do know," Brenda said, "is that Harvey and Stephanie's deaths were premeditated. Mrs. Bride and Officer Lomas, however, seemed to be spur of the moment. They weren't posed like the first two victims. Mrs. Bride was similar to them, but not quite the same. Her dress was up around her waist and her hands were positioned like Stephanie's."

"Was she sexually assaulted?" I asked, starting to feel sick to my stomach.

"No, but she wasn't posed, that's for sure. And Officer Lomas' body was sprawled all over the steps. Of course, his was a murder that hadn't been planned. He was just at the wrong place at the wrong time," Ed explained.

"Whatever happened to that piece of material he tore off the killer's jacket?"

"Forensics is still working that issue. So far, it hasn't provided much evidence that we can link to a suspect."

"Anything useful come off the hospital cameras? Why do you think he didn't try to pose my body like he did the others? If he'd tried, he'd have known it was pillows he shot, instead of me."

"I think he was concerned about time," Ed continued. "With Harvey, Stephanie, and Mrs. Bride he was alone with the bodies and thought he had the time to follow his ritual. In your hospital room he didn't know who would show up. You know how it is in a hospital, people come and go at all hours of the day and night and then there was Officer Lomas. As for the hall cameras leading to your room, he eluded them. However, he didn't know about the cameras in the stairwell. But then, we figure he hadn't planned on leaving that way until Officer Lomas starting chasing him. That's our best lead so far.

"We know exactly how tall Officer Lomas was and what he weighed. We're sure that the killer is tall, at least 5 feet 11 inches, because he was the same height as Lomas. Weight, though, is different. The killer weighs much less than Lomas. Our killer is tall and slender, but at this point that's all we've got. No idea what his motive is. Of course, if you'd told us about the will at the beginning, May, we would have gone down that road a lot sooner."

"I understand that what I did was stupid, but it wasn't done on purpose. All I can say to defend myself is that I was in shock, sick, medicated beyond belief, and scared. Something else I know you've thought about, your 'tall, slender' description fits Dickie Patty exactly."

Brenda and Ed looked at each other and I realized I'd said something they hadn't considered. I felt like I was sticking my nose where it didn't belong, even if it was my life on the line. This certainly wasn't the way a trained, professional police detective should feel, like a fish out of water. One minute I tell them I'm scared and the next I remind them about suspects they've overlooked. I got up ready to go, before it got worse. I was on the verge of crying again and I knew that would drive Ed crazy.

"Well, I'll leave. Thanks for your help. Keep me informed, okay? I'm going to Tacoma in the next day or so, but I'll leave my flight information and where I'm staying with you."

I started toward the door and Brenda touched my shoulder. I turned to her. She put her arms around me and I sobbed onto her spotless, white blouse.

After I'd calmed down and washed my face, I went out to my car and sat there for a couple of minutes. I pulled my cell phone out of my purse and called Janet. She wasn't in, so I left a message on her voice mail. I wanted to see if she and Frankie were doing okay, and to make sure Whiskers was still being a polite houseguest.

Ed and Brenda had tried to get me to stay longer, but all I wanted was to get away as fast as I could. It seemed the killer was pushing every emotional button I had. Ed told me to keep the vest on, as Janet had recommended. Again, I promised I would.

I didn't know if she was still in town, but I called Anne at the number she gave me. She answered on the first ring.

"Hello?"

"Hi, Anne. It's May. I wasn't sure if you'd gone back to Reno or not."

"Not yet. I've still got business in town."

"Did you get a chance to talk to your real estate friend about property in Pahrump yet?"

"As a matter of fact, I did."

"Great, some good news in my life. Would you like to have lunch, my treat, and we can talk about it? I need some girlfriend time."

"I'd like to do that, but I'm being a tourist in Boulder City today. Would you mind driving out here?" she asked.

It was about a thirty-minute drive to Boulder City, gateway to Hoover Dam and Lake Mead, but I enjoyed it. Anne had spent the morning touring the massive dam. Boulder City is one of those little gems in Nevada that tourists stumble over when they trek out to see Hoover Dam and Lake Mead. It reminds me of a green, pleasant New England town, except that it's surrounded by high desert and is next to an enormous man-made dam and lake. It was created during the 1930's when construction crews needed a place to live while they built the dam. Gambling isn't allowed in Boulder City and tourists flock to the area for the recreational activities on and around Lake Mead and Hoover Dam.

Anne was waiting for me at the restaurant she'd suggested. Her hair was pulled back in a chignon and it emphasized the high cheekbones and brown eyes that made her appearance so striking.

"You look beautiful with your hair that way," I said.

"Thank you. This is what I do when I haven't washed it."

"Yeah, one of our tricks, huh? That's one thing about short hair like mine, though, you can't change it around much. Maybe that's why I change the color."

"The red looks good. You should keep that one."

"I will. I'm enjoying my redhead period."

We laughed and chatted. She, as always, ordered the healthy stuff on the menu. I ordered a double cheeseburger, onion rings, and a chocolate shake.

"I don't see how you can eat like that and stay so thin," she commented, as she took a small bit of salad.

"It's because I don't eat on a regular basis. I honestly can't recall when I last had an actual meal. I eat on the run. Sometimes I don't eat at all."

"That can't be healthy. Your body is a machine and you need to keep it running smoothly. That means the right kind of fuel."

"You're beginning to sound like a doctor."

"I am a doctor," she said with a small laugh.

"Yeah, I know, but you don't work on 'live' people."

"That's true," she agreed. "But I still know what's good for you and eating like you do isn't good."

"How much longer will you be in town?" I asked, anxious to get off the topic of how I should eat.

"Not too much longer. I've almost finished my business in Las Vegas. Here's the information on who to call in Pahrump." She handed me a piece of paper with a name and number written on it. "He's the guy who worked with my former lover to find the property."

"Sounds like you should have kept that man in your life."

"I would have, but he left me for another woman."

"I can't believe any man would leave you. He must have been nuts."

"He said he liked me, wanted to be friends, but that a woman he used to know needed him. So he left. Then he got married."

"That must have broken your heart."

"Well, you know the old saying, 'if it doesn't kill you, it'll make you stronger'."

"Did it?"

"I'm not dead, am I?"

"No, ma'am, you look really healthy to me. I didn't see your rental car out front. Are you in the back parking lot?"

"I'm in the front. I've changed cars, though. The other one didn't seem to be working properly so I took it back."

"When did you do that?"

"The day after we drove out to Pahrump."

"I didn't notice anything wrong with that car. But I saw a car just like yours when I went out to see my lawyer in Summerlin."

"All rental cars look alike."

"I've heard that before," I replied.

"What's going on with the case?" Anne asked, as she picked at her shrimp salad.

"I just left Ed and Brenda. They don't seem to be making any progress. I talked with Dr. Williams earlier and he told me all four victims had been stunned before being shot. I was upset that no one told me. I mean, think about it. I'm the one the killer is after. Anyway, now that I know, I'm wearing my vest."

"Some of the new stun guns aren't stopped by vests," she replied.

"I know. I feel like a sitting duck."

"You should come to Sedona until this is cleared up," she said. "In fact, I'm driving to Arizona after I leave the restaurant."

"Thanks for asking. Right now, though, I need to get this situation sorted out."

"We could have a great time in Sedona. It would be a wonderful place for you to get your nerves under control."

"You're right and I wish I could just drop everything and go, but I can't. I'm glad I got to know you, Anne. You can't have too many friends, can you?"

We chatted a little while longer, I paid the bill, and then we went out to our cars. I noticed that her car was larger this time and the tag was from California. As police officers are trained to do from day one, I memorized her number on the spot.

"Thanks for having lunch with me, Anne. Keep in touch, if we don't see each other before you go back to Reno."

"We'll see each other again. And thank you for buying lunch," she said.

We got into our cars and headed in different directions. She drove south toward Arizona and the mystical town of Sedona.

By taking back streets I managed to miss the freeway clog, which had already started. I got to David's house just in time to answer the phone.

"Hello?"

"I've been calling you all afternoon. I'll be late tonight because I just got a booking. Do you want to fly along? It's beautiful over the canyon at dusk."

"I'll pass, David. But, please, let's do that another time. Actually, I have to pack. I'm going to Tacoma for a couple of days and if I know my lawyer, he'll have us on the next plane out of here."

"You mean you're leaving me already? You just moved in."

"It's only for a few days. I have to take care of some personal things in Washington, and then if it's okay with you, I'd like to come back out here when I return. "

"Move in on a permanent basis, that's what I'd like."

"We just met. How can you talk that way?"

"I know a good thing when I see it and you are one. I haven't been this interested in a woman in a long time, May. I don't intend to lose you."

"I'm high maintenance, I'm afraid."

"I don't think so. You've just been out in the cold too long by yourself. I want to keep you warm and safe."

"Can you see my smile through the phone line?"

"I sure can, and when we make love, you'll really smile."

"Something to look forward to, then." I felt a pleasant anticipation.

"You can bet on it," he replied.

# Nineteen

Just as I thought, Rick had wasted no time in getting us booked on a flight to Tacoma. He called with the information that I had just enough time to pack, shower, and drive to the airport. Our flight left at seven that evening.

"Couldn't we leave in the morning? Why do all this traveling at night?"

"You should have been to Tacoma last week. If we get there tonight, we can be at the law offices when they open tomorrow morning. I'm doing this in your interest, May."

"If you say so. I still don't half trust you, though."

"I know that. I intend to change your mind, but it will take a while, won't it?"

"You may never get me to change my mind, Rick. You're a dirty dog; just like Ed said the first time he met you."

"Ed isn't the one you should listen to when it comes to men, May. He's in love with you, too."

"He is not. We have a wonderful, platonic relationship."

"That's not what he really wants."

"You're nuts. I'm hanging up now. I'll see you at the airport."

I was just about to throw something in anger, when the phone rang again. "Hello!"

"You need to improve your communication skills, pal."

"Oh, Janet, thank heavens it's a woman. I'm getting sick-to-death of men. Do you hear me? Sick of all of them, except David."

"What's happened now?"

112

"Rick just told me that Ed loves me, in a carnal kind of way, and it infuriated me. Why does everybody think that I have something going on with my partners? I never do. Not with Harvey and certainly not with Ed. Why do people always seem to think that, Janet?"

"They're sort of right in a way."

"Wait a minute, you're supposed to be on my side."

"I am on your side, but I can explain this to you if you'll calm down."

"Has something happened to you or Frankie? Are you two all right? That's important stuff to talk about. I'm not sure this man-thing is."

"We're fine. And it is important to talk about because it did make you mad. Do you want to hear my theory?"

"I'm been hearing your theories on how to fix my life for a long time. Why stop now?"

"If you had a female partner, after a time, you'd love each other. Sort of like we love each other. If Ed had a male partner, he would love him. In dangerous jobs you depend, really staying-alive-depend, on your partner. It's normal. There is nothing aberrant about loving your partner. Rick is trying to turn it into a romantic sort of thing, even though he knows it's not, because he wants you for himself. He sees Ed as competition for you and he knows Ed dislikes him."

"How do you come up these theories?"

"It's human nature. Think about it and you'll agree it's true."

"Actually, I know you're right. Even Ed's wife knows that I have a strong bond with him. And Stephanie knew how it was with Harvey and me."

"I had a hard time with Tom when we first married, because back then most of my co-workers were men, and he didn't like that at all. We had some real issues to deal with over his jealousy. That's one reason we live apart."

"I never knew that."

"Even though Tom and I are a couple in our hearts, his jealousy drove me away, but I've never once been interested in any man except him."

"Is he still jealous of you, after all these years?"

"Not so much now. He's come to understand it better. Especially since so many women are in the Air Force now. He sees how it can be."

"How did you get so smart?"

"Good luck, I guess. Anyway, the real reason I called wasn't to psychoanalyze you, but to give you some news about the case."

"What is it?"

"Officer Lomas managed to rake some of his attacker's skin under his nails. Doc Williams found it during the autopsy. When we get a suspect, we can nail him with it. Also, have you heard about the guns?"

"Guns? As in more than one?"

"That's right. The killer has used a different type of gun and shells for each murder."

"Wait a minute. You mean Harvey and Stephanie were killed with different weapons?"

"Yes. The only ones that match are the shots fired into your pillows at the hospital, and Officer Lomas."

"That's because the killer was surprised. He didn't expect Lomas to chase him down. I've heard of killers using different weapons, but I've never had a case where it happened. Have you, Janet?"

"No, I haven't. It says volumes about the killer, though."

"It tells me he has an arsenal, and is familiar with all sorts of guns," I replied.

"It's also a game. He's playing with us. He knows what we look for and at every opportunity he's sending us down wrong paths. This is one clever dude," she said.

"Thanks so much for letting me know. Brenda and Ed haven't been very forthcoming with information for me. If it hadn't been for you, I wouldn't even have known to wear my vest."

"They have their orders, May, you know that. I'm outside their chain of command, so nobody has told me to keep it mum."

"You know, I've changed my mind about Brenda. She's a darn good detective."

"I know. I'm glad you got past the young and pretty part to recognize that."

"That jealousy thing, huh?"

"Yep. That stuff is toxic and will do you in. It's a big waste of time, too."

"I sure am glad you put up with me."

"We love each other, so it's okay. You have a safe trip to Tacoma. And don't forget that this guy has weapons of every size and type. Don't take anything or anyone for granted. How about calling me when you get there? I worry about you. I'll hang up now."

I thought about what Janet had told me as I packed. Janet had more common sense in her thumbnail than I did in my entire body. What she'd told me was frightening, but I'd rather know about it than not. The killer was an expert in all sorts of pistols.

To get my mind away from guns and murder, I worried about what to take with me. Since I was heading for a colder climate, I threw in a couple of heavy sweaters that I keep for nighttime in the desert. It gets cold fast in Las Vegas, though that's something the tourists don't hear about too often. When the sun falls below the mountains, the temperature drops like a rock. In Tacoma, sweaters could be used throughout the year, day and night. I remember the town fondly, but don't miss the climate at all.

The drive to McCarran International Airport was uneventful. I parked my car in the airport garage and took an elevator to the check in area. I was to meet Rick near the airline we were booked on to fly to Tacoma. He wasn't there, which surprised me, so I waited around impatiently for him to show up. I've always liked the Las Vegas airport. It's cheerful, with its bright colors and the constant "ching, ching" of the slot machines. The music that's played throughout the airport is upbeat, toe tapping and makes me want to boogey. I even liked the metallic palm trees that towered above people as they walk the concourses to get to their flights.

After I'd checked my watch for the twentieth time, I pulled out my phone and called Rick's office. No one answered, which wasn't too surprising, since it was after office hours. I left him a message and put my phone back in my purse. I finally decided I'd better check in without him. He'd probably got caught in traffic. I'd tried to talk him out of going at this time of day, but he wouldn't listen. It would be fun teasing him about it, when he showed up.

I stood in the short line, got to the clerk, and checked my bag. I don't like carrying any sort of bag onto the airline. I like to travel light and hauling luggage around an airport isn't my idea of fun. I figure if it gets lost, I'll buy new stuff at my destination. Anyway, I've never once had a bag lost by an airline, so I don't worry about it.

The check-in clerk was friendly, organized, and very professional. I told her that Rick should be along any minute and she said he had plenty of time. That reassured me as I took my boarding pass and began the long walk to the gate. Since I had time, I went into several of the shops that lined the walkway. I bought a few Las Vegas oriented items for friends I would see in Tacoma, and bought a paperback romance to keep me awake during the flight. I must have read a thousand of those romance novels over the years. I loved how they ended so prettily, totally unlike any romance in my life.

I got to the gate and sat down to wait for Rick. Usually I enjoy sitting in the airport and watching people. This time, though, I felt nervous. I couldn't even get interested when a lady with a pet carrier sat across from me. Most times I get down on all fours and coo at whatever little animal is inside. People walked past loaded down with slices of pizza, hamburgers, hot dogs, fries, ice cream, pastries, and coffee cups galore. I couldn't even get interested in a cup of coffee. After a few more nervous minutes, I pulled out my phone and called Rick's office. Still no answer so I left another message. I called Ed and left him a message as well. By then, boarding had started for my flight. I couldn't believe my lawyer had stood me up.

The flight didn't take long, under two hours. I kept busy with my romance novel and spent a little time talking with my seatmates. They were an older couple who had come down from Seattle to visit their quarter acre lot in one of the new subdivisions that seemed to spring up overnight.

"We try to visit at least twice a year. Someday we'll build a house on it and enjoy that sunshine you have here in Nevada," the man told me. His wife, who looked very tired and older than her husband, agreed that it would be a dream come true when they could move to the Las Vegas area permanently.

I almost told them to go ahead and move and not to wait, because you never know what's coming, but I decided to nod politely in agreement, and not give unsolicited advice. Maybe I was getting smarter as I got older.

Since it was past nine in the evening, I couldn't see Mount Rainier as we approached Seattle-Tacoma International Airport. I love to see that snow-capped, craggy, majestic peak. When I first arrived in Tacoma, it had taken two weeks before the weather cleared enough that I could see "the mountain." It was worth the wait. When the sun shines, the Puget Sound region is the most beautiful place I've ever lived. But there's a catch. Sunshine is elusive in the Pacific Northwest.

The plane taxied down the runway and came to a stop outside the lit up windows of the terminal. It had only been a few months since I'd been here. My last trip was joyous and I arrived from Las Vegas full of happiness for Harvey and Stephanie. They'd had a magical wedding. It was held outside in the Japanese Garden at Point Defiance Park in North Tacoma. It wasn't far from where my house had been located. I used to jog the Park's five-mile drive on a regular basis. Stephanie had been perfect in her beige, lace dress and matching jacket. Harvey was handsome in a black tuxedo. At Stephanie's request, I wore a pink knee-length dress that was similar, but not as elaborate, to the one she wore. It had been one of those dream days, with weather so perfect we could see the Olympic and Cascade mountain ranges in all their snow-capped glory. In every direction mountains surrounded us, but Mount Rainier, at over fourteen thousand feet, dominated.

From certain areas, you could actually see Mount Baker, which is near the Canadian border. Commencement Bay was calm and a beautiful dark blue. Sailboats bobbed gently on the water. Motorboats roared around the bay and if they came close to shore, we could hear them as they broke the peaceful silence of the Japanese Garden.

It had been a small wedding, less than fifty guests, but it was the most memorable and beautiful event I have ever attended. What made it so special was that Harvey and Stephanie clearly loved each other. Stephanie carried a single red rose, but the gardens were filled with flowers of every color and type. The azaleas, tulips, and rhododendrons were spectacular. The largest daffodils I had ever seen stood as sentinels, their huge yellow heads basking in the warm sun. Afterwards, we went to the Tacoma Yacht Club for the reception. Harvey had looked so happy and pleased with himself. Stephanie glowed as she held onto his arm, glancing up at him constantly, the love evident in her eyes.

I was so lost in remembering that I had to be nudged to get up so my seatmates could get out. I smiled, apologized for holding them up, and got out of their way as they collected their bags.

"Enjoy your visit," the man said. He was certainly the more communicative of the two, his wife stood silently behind him in the line that snaked toward the exit door.

"I'll do my best," I replied. "And maybe you ought to just go ahead and move to Las Vegas, since that's really where you want to live." I couldn't resist saying it. The wife looked at me and finally I saw a spark in her eyes.

"I've been telling him that for five years. Maybe he'll listen to you, because he certainly won't to me."

"I listen, Harriet," he said in his defense. "We just don't have our retirements settled yet. When we do we'll move."

I could tell by the wife's dejected look that she had heard that excuse more than once.

# Twenty

Seattle-Tacoma International Airport was colored in muted shades, mostly grays and blues. I saw lights reflected in the rain puddles on the tarmac through the large glass windows. People were dressed in dark colored clothes, some of them with puffy down jackets that put twenty pounds on everyone who wore them. Many had backpacks, which made them look like camels with humps.

Department of Transportation home security employees were everywhere. They were easy to spot with their white shirts sporting patriotic shoulder patches. Flight attendants walked by, all cheery chatter and sensible heels. The soothing music that pumped throughout the airport matched the subdued colors and tone, but it didn't make me want to dance. Wonderful coffee aromas tempted me as I approached the main concourse. One of these days when I had time, I'd drink all the lattes I wanted. I'd sit someplace, preferably in a warm climate, not worry about anything and drink lattes with lots of whipped cream.

It didn't take long to retrieve my bag and I was on my way to the car rental area when I heard my name called. I turned around and found myself facing a young man who had a sign with my name on it.

"Are you May Scott?" he politely inquired.

"Yes."

"I'm your driver, Ronnie Catrel. Let me take your bag. Would you please wait outside while I get the car? I'll pick you up in five minutes. They won't let us leave the cars at the curb anymore. Sorry for the inconvenience."

"Who sent you? How did you know who I was?"

"I work for Bush, Catrel, and Smith. The lawyers you'll be seeing tomorrow. I do all sorts of jobs for them and I'm going to school to be a lawyer myself someday. My uncle is Albert Catrel, the one in the middle. That's what he calls himself, 'The one in the middle'. Mr. Purdue gave my uncle your description."

"I had no idea I'd have a driver. Have you heard from Rick Purdue? He was supposed to be on this flight with me."

"No, I haven't heard from him, but he's the attorney my uncle has been working with to get you here. I wasn't sure if Mr. Purdue was coming, but we've been expecting you for several days."

"Yes, I know. And Rick tried to get me here sooner, but there have been complications." I didn't intend to go into a detailed description of the last few days. It was hard to believe all that had happened—and that I managed to live through it.

The car that Ronnie pulled up to the curb was beautiful. It was a cream-colored Lincoln with wonderful soft leather seats. I sat in the back, at Ronnie's insistence, but it made me feel awkward. Before we drove out of the terminal, I asked him to pull over so I could ride up front with him.

"I'm not used to being chauffeured around."

"I can tell." Ronnie turned his head toward me and smiled as he said it. "You aren't the typical rich client. And you're definitely not the lawyer type. To tell you the truth, I'm not sure if I am, either."

"Lawyers are a different breed, aren't they?"

"My uncle is a great guy, don't get me wrong. And I like Mr. Purdue, too. But some of them are just dirt bags."

"I get the picture."

"I just don't want to be a lawyer like that."

"Ronnie, I have a feeling that would never happen. I think the ones you described don't realize they're like that."

"I think they know and simply don't care."

"I'm looking forward to meeting your uncle. I've met a few of the partners while there with Harvey, but never Mr. Catrel, 'the one in the middle', as you described him."

"You'll like him, everybody does. He's the best lawyer in Tacoma, too. I've heard lots of people say that and not just because he's my uncle."

We chatted back and forth, and because it was late, traffic on I-5 flowed easily. We got to the Tacoma City Center exit in about fifteen minutes. On a bad commute day, the drive could have taken two hours.

The Tacoma Dome, with its wooden roof and intricately painted mountain peaks in shades of blue, was on our right as we headed into downtown. The first time I'd seen the Dixie Chicks in concert had been in the Dome.

Soon after we passed the steel cabled Twenty-first Street Bridge, which forms a mountain shape, The Glass Museum came into view. It was easy to spot because of its distinctive tilted, conical shaped Hot Shop Amphitheater. Someday I wanted to go in and watch the glass blowers create their art, but that would have to be on another visit.

We drove under the pedestrian overpass, named the Chihuly Bridge of Glass, with its beautiful glass art works in full display. The walkway connected downtown to the Glass Museum and the Thea Foss Waterway esplanade.

To the left of the walkway, the renovated Union Station housed the Federal Courthouse, where Harvey and I had spent many long hours. I caught a glimpse of the University of Washington-Tacoma branch, which was located across the street from the courthouse. It seemed that each time I returned to Tacoma, the university had built or renovated another building as they continued to march up the hillside.

The city had dipped back into its own history and brought back a version of the cable cars that used to ferry people around town. The new trams that run on silent tracks are a state-of-the-art light rail system. They reminded me of old photos of Tacoma when cable cars used to operate on these same hilly streets.

As we passed the grand piano shaped Tacoma Art Museum, I

realized we'd missed the street that led to the Sheraton Hotel.

"Hey, driver, you missed your turn," I said as Ronnie whipped down Schuster Parkway heading toward the Ruston Way Waterfront.

"You don't want to stay in a hotel when you have that nice house in the North End, do you?" he asked, clearly puzzled.

"I sold that nice house, Ronnie. Harvey took care of that for me. In fact, he used your uncle's law firm. I don't think the current owners would appreciate me showing up on their doorstep."

Ronnie looked at me in confusion. "You don't know, do you?"

"Know what?" I asked.

"I'll just let you see for yourself," he said.

We drove onto Ruston Way and I watched as people walked and jogged along the well-lighted sidewalks that bordered Commencement Bay. I used to do the same thing, and like them, in any type of weather. After a mile, we turned left and wound our way up a steep, heavily treed switchback road. It led to the street that used to be my old neighborhood.

Many of the houses had spectacular views of the Bay and when the weather cooperated, Mount Rainier, the Cascade and Olympic Mountain Ranges with their snowcapped peaks. My former house had a little bit of a view, but not one that had forced me to pay extra taxes, like some of my previous neighbors endured.

I was surprised that nothing much had changed since I'd left. If anything, the area looked nicer than I remembered. I hadn't had time to visit the old neighborhood when I was in town for Harvey and Stephanie's wedding a few months ago.

When we got to the house, it looked the same, sort of, but there were obvious changes. For one thing, someone who knew what they were doing had landscaped the yard. There was a low, white picket fence around the front with a pretty trellised gate. It looked like a rose bush was growing up and over, but it might be some other plant. I couldn't tell in the darkness. A beautifully formed Japanese maple tree gracefully stood to the left of a new front porch. Ronnie slowed the car in front of the house, then eased around to the right side and pulled onto the driveway. He pushed a button on the remote he held and the garage door opened. The car took up most of the room in the garage, but there was certainly enough room for us to get out. Since I had never had a garage, this was new to me.

"Why did you pull the car in here? And where are the people who bought the house?"

"I thought Rick had told you about the will, May. My uncle said you knew all about this, which obviously isn't true. Let's go inside and I'll explain, as much as I know, anyway."

Ronnie took a key out of his jacket pocket and opened a door that I hadn't noticed. We walked though a small hallway that housed a washer-dryer combination and a deep sink. Ronnie flipped the light switch and I looked around in amazement at what had once been my cramped, dark kitchen.

It looked like a kitchen I had seen in magazines, but never in real life. Maple cabinets graced the walls and a stainless steel double oven gleamed. In fact, all the appliances were stainless steel. The wood floors matched the cabinets. There was a small colorful rug on the floor and a garden window contained blooming African violets, my favorite. A small round table with two chairs sat in an alcove in front of a large, multi-paned window. Next to the new window, a pair of French doors opened onto a brick paved patio. A mantled fireplace stood against one wall.

"The owners have certainly changed this house. This used to be two rooms, but now that it's one, it's opened up the whole inside. And look at that yard. It's beautiful." I unlocked and stepped through the French doors and gazed in amazement at the changes that had been made. The house backed up to a ravine, so it had always been private, but the yard had never been landscaped. It was amazing what brick walkways, grass, a small fountain, trees and plants could do for a yard.

I came back in and walked through the rest of the fully furnished house. The master bedroom had been enlarged with the additions of a walk in closet and a fantastic bathroom. A jetted tub was situated next to a window that overlooked a small private garden. The shower stall was formed of curved, etched glass.

"Ronnie, this is the most beautiful bathroom I've ever seen. But why does it look so unlived in? Where are the owners?"

"Look in the mirror," he said.

"Look in the mirror? Why should I do that?" I asked, as I looked in the mirror.

"That's the owner of this house that you're looking at."

I turned to face him and finally realized what had been in front of me all along. "Harvey bought my house from me?" I asked, tears beginning to course down my face.

"Yes. Then he fixed it up and put it in the will that you were to have it when he passed away. Didn't Mr. Purdue tell you this stuff?"

"I need to go sit down." I wiped the tears from my face and tried to get my emotions under control. Harvey had loved me so much and I hadn't realized the full extent until he died. My heart broke with the thought that I would never get to tell him how much I had loved him, too.

We went back into the kitchen and I pulled out one of the pretty chairs and sat. I put my head in my hands and rubbed my temples. "Now that you mention it, Rick did give me a big package that I was supposed to read through and then talk with him about. But I never read it and never asked him about it. In his office, he told me about real estate that would come to me, but I guess I wasn't paying that much attention. I was in such grief over Harvey and Stephanie that I just couldn't take it in. What you're telling me is that I still own this house?"

"Free and clear."

"Why did Harvey fix it up?"

"He said it was a labor of love. He did all the yard work himself, but contracted out the rest of it. In fact, I helped him with the yard. Do you like it?"

"Like it? It's beautiful. It's overwhelming what Harvey did for me out of love. Maybe you should consider another career option instead of law. How about Master Gardener?"

"No. It was fun and relaxing, but I guess the law is in my genes."

"I need to read that will and see exactly what's in there, don't I?"

My emotions were raw, and everywhere I looked in this beautiful house, I saw Harvey's love for me.

"You can do that tomorrow. Could you come down to the office in the morning around nine? You know where it's located, don't you?"

"Yes, in fact, I've been there with Harvey. Will you pick me up?"

Ronnie smiled as he pulled keys out of his pocket. "This set is for the house. And this set is for your car – the one that's parked in the garage. My ride is parked across the street. I'll see you in the morning."

I thanked him for all he had done and went to the window, in the living room, to watch as he pulled away from the curb in his black, shiny truck. I walked around the house again and looked at how different it was. I liked the furniture Harvey, and maybe Stephanie, had selected. The refrigerator was filled with food and drinks so I took a soda. I'd have to ask Ronnie tomorrow about the furniture and the food. I guessed he'd done the grocery shopping for me when he found out I was actually going to arrive.

The thing that perplexed me was that Harvey had never said a word to me about any of this. Why in the world he didn't tell me I didn't think I'd ever understand. Unless, of course, one of the lawyers I'd see in the morning could fill in the blanks for me. Lawyers were good at that fill-in-the-blank stuff and I never had been.

I called Rick at his office and left another message. I knew he wouldn't be at work at this time of the night and I didn't want to call him at home. I did the same with Ed and Brenda, just to let them know I'd arrived safely.

The house was so pretty that I was afraid to touch anything, which was strange, because it belonged to me. I got over it when I took off my clothes and got into the wonderful jetted tub. In fact, I fell asleep in the warm water. When I woke up I felt better. I toweled off and padded into the bedroom to dig through my bag for my nightshirt. After I put it on, I walked through the house again and because I was hungry, searched through the kitchen for something to eat. I found popcorn so I put that in the microwave. Then I got the ice cream from the freezer and scooped up a large bowl. I had a wonderful dinner, salty and sweet. After I'd eaten and put my various bowls and spoons in the dishwasher, I was tired.

The bed looked so tempting. Originally I thought I'd sleep on the couch but it seemed ridiculous. I had to get used to the idea that what had once been my house still was. I pulled the covers back, set my clock to make sure I made the meeting and crawled into bed. I fell asleep instantly and slept better than I had in a long time. I felt safe and was beginning to feel at home, wrapped in Harvey's love.

# Twenty-one

I woke up before the alarm went off. I took a quick shower, washed my hair and put on my clothes. I realized I should start dressing nicer now that I had money, this house and the Lincoln parked in the garage. My surroundings had gone upscale but I hadn't. It was too early for shops to be open so people would just have to deal with me in my wrinkled pants and baggy sweater. At least my shoes looked nice.

I put together a pot of coffee, made toast with lots of butter, and turned on the TV to watch the local news. I flipped through the stations until I found a face I recognized. I sat down, drank several cups of coffee, ate my toast and luxuriated in my surroundings. I began to understand what Harvey had been trying to tell me, that I needed to have a life away from my job. I'd never done that. As I looked around this quiet, lovely room with the sun pouring in making everything sparkle, I felt at peace. It reminded me of something David had said to me recently. "You've been out in the cold too long by yourself. I want to keep you warm and safe." I think that's what Harvey had wanted for me, too.

I was about to walk out the door on the way to my appointment when my cell phone rang. I pulled it out of my purse and flipped it open.

"Hello," I said.

"May, its Ed. Where are you right now?" He sounded worried.

"I'm in my old house in the North End of Tacoma. Wait until you hear – Harvey bought it from me, fixed it up, and left it to me in his

127

will. Can you believe that?"

"Listen to me, May. Slow down and listen. Your lawyer has been murdered."

"You mean the lawyer I'm about to go see has been murdered?"

"No, Rick Purdue was shot through the head late yesterday afternoon. His assistant found him this morning when she came to work. She said she was surprised to see his car at work so early, since he usually didn't come in until around nine."

That explained why Rick had missed the plane. I went to the couch and sat down.

"Is this ever going to stop, Ed?"

"Yes, it will. But I need you to be very cautious. Do you hear me?"

"Do you think the killer is in Tacoma?"

"I don't know, May. There seems to be some items missing from Rick's desk and from the looks of it, it was your file that was spread all over the top. He must have been getting ready for the meeting with you and those Washington lawyers."

"Do you know what was taken?"

"His assistant is going over it right now. We've only been here a few minutes. I called you just as soon as I saw the body. Did you take your vest to Tacoma? How about your Beretta?"

"No, I didn't."

"Okay, then go to your old station and borrow a vest and a gun while you're there. Just as soon as we know what this jerk took, I'll call. I'll be calling the Tacoma Police Department as soon as I hang up. Is there a particular person you want me to deal with, May? Any old buddy that you trust?"

I leaned my head into my hand and rubbed my temples. "Let me think."

"I don't have time for you to think. Yes or no?"

"No, I can't think of anybody right now. Harvey was that person."

"Okay, I'll call you with any news and who I'm dealing with in Tacoma. When are you coming back to Las Vegas?"

"Tomorrow morning. I should be back in the office before noon."

"I'll make sure I'm here. You be careful, May. I'll be calling as soon as I know anything else," he said and hung up.

I looked at my watch and realized I needed to leave in order to get to my appointment. It was hard for me to move. I hadn't known Rick that long, but he'd changed my life. I'd shortened his; because he'd come into my life, he was now dead. This was getting to be way too much.

After a few moments I got up, went out to the garage and used the remote to open the door. I hadn't driven a car like this before, at least not one that I owned. I got in, turned on the ignition and the power of it reminded me of the big, ugly unmarked police car Ed and I drove in Las Vegas. There was nothing ugly about this car, though.

I drove down the steep, curved road and turned right onto Ruston Way. Because the morning was crystal clear, sunny and beautiful the sidewalks were crowded. Joggers, walkers, most with their dogs leading the way, and skaters competed for space. A few people were trying to fly kites, but the wind wasn't cooperating. Several piers jutted out into the bay and hopeful anglers tossed their lines into the calm, brackish water. Though it was early and a weekday, sailboats dotted the horizon. Vashon Island and Brown's Point, with its small lighthouse, looked serene. The ferry from Point Defiance to Vashon Island was halfway across the bay on one of its many scheduled roundtrip crossings. Volcanic Mount Rainier towered over everything and I could understand why early Indian tribes had considered it a sacred place. It made a spectacular backdrop for hilly Tacoma. I'd often wondered why this view of the city wasn't used in advertising because it showed Commencement Bay, Tacoma, and Mount Rainier at their most stunning.

I followed the curved shoreline of Commencement Bay downtown and veered right into the city. I didn't have to go very far because the law offices were located in the clock towered building called Old City Hall which as the name implied, was its history. I made a left turn a little way past the building and parked on a side street across from the elegant red brick and glass Frank Russell Building.

I got out of the car, locked it, and walked the short distance to Old

City Hall. The Law Offices of Bush, Catrel, and Smith were located on the ground level of the building so I could enter from the street. I opened the heavy, dark door and went inside.

The office was different than Rick's. This office had been around for a long time and I could smell 'old money' in the air. The furnishings were leather, dark wood, and expensive Oriental touches that included a beautiful multicolored Chinese rug. I remembered it from my visits with Harvey. It was quiet in the office; even the ringing phones were muted. The conservative law firm reminded me of Harvey; low key and quietly powerful.

The well-dressed young man at the reception desk took my name and called back to one of the many offices. He spoke into the small microphone on the headset he wore as he continued to work at the computer.

"Ms. Scott, please go down this hall," he indicated to the left. "It's the first office on the left. Mr. Catrel is waiting for you."

I walked down the carpeted hall and my footsteps were muffled. Unlike Rick's offices, which were filled with glass and light, privacy would be assured here. Closed doors and the lack of windows made me claustrophobic. I longed to be anywhere, but here. I felt light-headed. I stopped for a moment and leaned down toward my knees, trying to regain composure. Slowly I rose and felt cold sweat cover my body. I looked up and realized I was directly in front of Mr. Catrel's office. I knocked and opened the door.

The small room had enough space for a desk with an attractive, young assistant behind it, several upholstered chairs and a table with current magazines. Brass floor lamps with a dragon design etched onto the metal, cast soft circles of light next to the chairs. I could see the hand of an interior designer who had made the most efficient use of the available space, while keeping it uncluttered and professional.

"Ms. Scott, Mr. Catrel is waiting for you. Just go right in," Angela said. I knew her name and position because of the rosewood nameplate on her mahogany desk.

I lightly knocked on the door to his office and he opened it immediately. He put his hand out to shake mine and said, "I'm so sorry to hear about your situation. Please come in, Ms. Scott."

Albert Catrel looked like a much older version of his nephew, Ronnie. Both of them were slight with thinning hair. Like Ronnie, his uncle had an open, friendly face which is a tremendous asset for a lawyer. His suit was tailored to fit his small stature. At 5'1", I understood the benefits and drawbacks of being petite. However, for a man, it must present even more disadvantages. I wondered if the old axiom about the "Napoleon Complex" would be true for Albert Catrel, Attorney-at-Law. I also wondered if he'd heard about Rick's murder.

A quick glance around his office left no doubt that appearance mattered a great deal to him. His office melded together the best of Old World and Asian elegance, plus up-to-date technology, evidenced by the small computer notebook on top of his enormous rosewood desk. Two upholstered chairs sat in front of his desk with Tiffany style floor lamps on either side. Photos of sailing ships graced the walls on each side of the furniture and the theme was echoed on the tall bookshelf to the right of his desk. Matched sets of law books marched up the bookcase, with sailing ship models and Oriental vases of various sizes and shapes adding touches of brilliant color. The colors from the vases were reflected in the rug that covered most of the oak floor.

"I thought the rug you have in the lobby was exquisite, but this one is even lovelier," I said, trying to buy time.

He smiled and directed me to one of two dark leather club chairs that sat in the right corner of his office, next to a floor to ceiling window. A vertical blind covered the window but still let in an amazing amount of light. A small, round glass-topped rosewood coffee table with writhing dragons carved onto the base sat in front of the chairs.

"Is this too bright for you?" he asked. "I can close it, if you prefer."

"No, actually it will make me feel better to have sunlight pouring in. I've been putting off asking you, but have you heard about Rick Purdue?" I asked as I sat down on the soft leather.

"Yes, I have. I got a call from his assistant at the law firm this morning. It's a terrible situation and I want you to know we will help you with anything in our power."

I had a feeling that power would be considerable but I didn't say it out loud. I didn't feel as comfortable with this man as I had with Rick. I could hear Janet's dialog running through my head and I knew she wouldn't approve of how I'd sized up Albert Catrel. Of course, maybe I was doing this because Rick was dead and I didn't want to face the fact that his business relationship with me had caused it. Perhaps Mr. Catrel was nervous having me in his office. After all one of his oldest, best clients and a lawyer he knew and respected had both been recently murdered on my account.

"Could I offer you coffee or tea, Ms. Scott?" he asked.

"No, thank you, I've had several cups this morning."

"I understand from Ronnie that you aren't too well versed in the will that we drew up with Harvey."

"No, I'm afraid I'm not very diligent when it comes to paperwork, Mr. Catrel."

"Please, call me Albert."

"And I'm May."

He smiled and it seemed genuine. Maybe my reservations about him, first impressions based on appearance, were incorrect. On the other hand, someone was out to kill me and I didn't know who it was or what his motive might be.

# Twenty-two

Albert and I spent the better part of the morning going over the will, step by step. He left no stone unturned. I discovered that I was wealthier than I'd imagined. The real estate holdings amazed me the most. Harvey had purchased parcels of real estate since he'd been a very young man. I glanced at the list and realized that I owned portions of downtown Tacoma, to include the building I was in. Harvey and Stephanie had built a home on a golf course in the Gig Harbor community, about ten miles from Tacoma, which now belonged to me.

"I thought Harvey and Stephanie were going to move to Las Vegas, but after reading about all this real estate, I guess they never intended to do that."

"No, he did intend to move down there, at least in the winter months. Then they'd come back to Gig Harbor for the summer. His plan was to entice you to do the same. That's why he purchased and renovated the North End house for you."

"So that was the plan. Why didn't he tell me about it?"

"Part of it was he wanted it to be a surprise. The other part was he wasn't sure you'd do it."

"That was a correct assumption on his part. I'm not sure I'd do that now, either. I like living in Nevada. The heat doesn't bother me – but cold does. Even the summers here aren't warm enough for me."

I continued to look through the sheets of paper that listed the various holdings in several states. "What's this in Nevada?" I asked, as I read a property description that might as well have been in Greek.

Albert took the page and looked at it. "It's fifty acres in a place called Pahrump."

"Where do you see that?"

"Here," he pointed to a section that listed the name.

"Where is it in Pahrump?"

"From this legal description, it's on the north side."

I wondered if it was close to Anne's property. That, too, had been on the north side. What do you know; I wouldn't have to use Anne's real estate contact. I already owned property in Pahrump.

"Now that we've gone over the will thoroughly do you want me to go with you to open the safety deposit box?"

"Is it here in Tacoma?"

"No, it's at the bank Harvey used in Gig Harbor."

"If it had been downtown, I'd have gone alone. But I don't know much about Gig Harbor. It's probably better that you go with me."

"I think that's wise. I can take you to see the home in Gig Harbor and the waterfront property on Fox Island that you own."

"This is overwhelming. I can't imagine that I own so much property. What in the world will I do with it?"

"You'll find something to do with it, I'm sure. This is a gift from a man who considered you to be his daughter. I know the circumstances are tragic, but you should consider yourself a lucky woman. Not many people have an opportunity like this."

He was right. I was lucky. However, Harvey, Stephanie, Mrs. Bride, Officer Lomas, and Rick had paid with their lives for my good fortune.

We agreed to meet back at the law firm after lunch. I wanted to visit the Tacoma Police Department and borrow a vest and gun. Ed hadn't called back and I was surprised. I called him but he didn't answer so I left a message.

The five-minute drive from Albert's office to the police station clarified how much had changed in Tacoma since I'd left eight years ago. There'd been a renaissance of the downtown area. New and renovated buildings, condominiums, apartments, sidewalk artwork, and innovative parks had created a livable and likable urban environment. Light rail linked the downtown streets with the commuter train to Seattle, which is located across from Freight House Square near the Tacoma Dome. I had to stop a couple of times to let the trams make their way down the track.

I pulled into the parking lot and found a space near the County-City Building. This, at least, looked familiar. I locked the car and walked toward the building where Harvey and I had first met. I looked up to the third floor window where our office used to be. When I entered the door I couldn't believe that the person working security was someone I recognized.

"Ted, is that you? You haven't changed a bit."

"Neither have you, Detective Scott. What brings you back here from 'Lost Wages'?"

"Sad business, I'm afraid. Did you hear that Harvey and Stephanie Jordan were murdered last week in Las Vegas?"

"Yes, and when I heard I immediately thought of the two of you and how good a detective team you were. There's been nobody here near as good as you and Harvey were. He was a fine man. I know you must be suffering from the loss of such a wonderful friend."

"You said exactly what's in my heart, Ted, and thank you for that. I thought you'd be retired by now."

"Soon. It'll be this year. The missus said I've worked long enough so she's going to let me put my paperwork in." He laughed, but there was truth in his words. I remembered his wife and how she made him toe the straight and narrow.

"I need to borrow a vest and a gun. Where do I do that, Ted?"

"Let me make a call and I'll send you first time to the right office. I don't like sending good folks like you on a wild goose chase."

True to his word, Ted sent me to Sergeant Nelson in Property Control. As I walked down the hall I felt like I'd never left. The building looked the same until I got to Property Control, which was listed on a sign outside an office. I peeped around the open door and said, "Didn't this used to be the cafeteria?"

"That's right," said Sergeant Nelson. "That's moved downstairs. The foods not any better, though."

"I liked the coffee and the chicken salad sandwiches."

"You must not eat much good food if you liked those menu items," Sergeant Nelson said with a shudder and a grin.

I walked into the office, put my hand out and said, "I'm Detective May Scott, Las Vegas Metro Police. I guess you know that I'm here to borrow a vest and a gun?"

"Yep. I was forewarned this morning. Your partner from Las Vegas called earlier. Sorry about the situation. I knew Detective Jordan, but I can't place you."

"I left about eight years ago. Harvey Jordan trained me right here in this building. Spent almost twelve years with him."

"He was a great guy. After all those years of being a cop, then he gets murdered right before he was to retire. I got an email about his retirement ceremony and the party afterwards just a few days ago. He was going to host a party for all of us at his place in Gig Harbor."

"Harvey was terrific."

"From what I've heard, you're not having an easy time of it either."

"It's been a rough few days. I don't know if I'll need this equipment but to be on the safe side I'll borrow it."

"No problem. And I don't blame you. I'd do the same thing. Come on back and I'll get you fixed up."

Twenty minutes later, I was back in my car fitted with a vest that had ceramic inserts and a Glock 9mm. I sat there for a couple of minutes and thought about getting something to eat. I decided I wasn't that hungry, started the car, and drove back to the law office. Albert was waiting for me and offered to drive to Gig Harbor.

We walked a block to his car. It surprised me that it was a small, fuel-efficient model. "I figured you'd have a Mercedes," I said as I got into the little car. "Harvey used to call a car like this a 'tin can'."

"Yes, he did. He favored large, eye-catching cars, which explains how you came to be the owner of a Lincoln. He thought they were safer."

"You'd think he would've preferred a car like this, knowing how he loved to pinch a penny."

"Harvey liked quality and didn't mind paying for it. I, on the other hand, like quality and do all I can to get the best value for the least amount of money."

We continued to chat and I looked with interest at the streets I'd known like the back of my hand a few years ago. Things had changed but I felt I could still make my way around Tacoma without getting lost.

New businesses that catered to the college crowd had cropped up on Sixth Avenue. The University of Puget Sound, where I'd taken night and weekend classes to get my degree in criminal justice, was a few blocks away. That had been a difficult time during my life because of the heavy work pressures I was under. Harvey had prodded me, though, and he's the reason that I completed the degree. He and his first wife, Vicki, attended my graduation. Afterwards, we'd gone to a celebration dinner at the Lobster Shop on Ruston Way. As I thought about all he had done to affect my life, tears streamed down my face. I tried to wipe them away before Albert saw but I wasn't successful.

"This must be a painful trip for you to make, May. It's my loss, too, Harvey and I were friends for years."

"It is a painful trip. I'm so sorry that Harvey, Stephanie, Mrs. Bride, Officer Lomas, and Rick died because of me. I wish I could give all this money and property back. It's not worth what they gave up."

"It's not your fault. You're not responsible. There's no telling why the killer did it but whatever the reason it'll be lunacy. You can't blame yourself for another person's actions."

"I just don't like the idea that I've profited by it. It seems wrong."

"If you'd coerced Harvey into setting up his will to benefit you and then murdered him and Stephanie, I'd be the first to agree with you. But, May, you had no idea any of this was going to happen and had zero control. You should view yourself as a victim."

"I don't like the sound of that. I'm not victim material."

"That's a comment I wholeheartedly agree with," Albert said.

"You'll survive this. And because Harvey cared so much for you, money won't be an issue. He wanted you to be happy. Look at the positive side. You can use your wealth to help those you love, just like Harvey did."

"You sound exactly like my friend Janet. Have you two been talking behind my back?"

He laughed and said 'no'. I began to understand why Harvey had trusted him; Harvey could recognize value, in a product or a person. Albert might be small in stature, but he was a large man in ways that mattered. Janet would be pleased I'd figured that out on my own without her prompting.

As we approached the on-ramp to Highway 16, construction equipment blocked part of the entranceway. "What's this?"

"This," he said, "is part of the road construction phase for the building of the second Narrows Bridge."

"They finally decided to build it, huh? That fight was going on when I lived here."

"Traffic has gotten so bad that something had to be done. Still, people aren't convinced it's the answer, especially since there'll be a toll on the bridge."

We pulled onto the highway, which was backed up with early afternoon traffic.

"This is what I remember about the Puget Sound area – sitting in traffic. I hope a second bridge will get rid of this congestion."

"Yes, it'll benefit the entire Peninsula area if that's the case."

"Do you live in Gig Harbor?"

"No. We used to live in the North End, not too far from your house. When our kids grew up we sold it and bought a condo in one of the new buildings near the Glass Museum. My wife teaches part-time at the University of Washington-Tacoma, so we can both walk to work."

"Do you keep your car at the garage near your office?"

"There's parking under the condo. I drove it in today because I figured you and I would be going to Gig Harbor."

Stop and go traffic made the ten-mile trip last about an hour. As soon as we got onto the Narrows Bridge, which looks like a smaller, green version of the red, Golden Gate Bridge in San Francisco, traffic speeded up. I enjoyed crossing the swirling, rough waters far below. The first bridge that was built on this site lasted three months. A violent windstorm tore the structure apart and it fell to a watery grave. Divers liked to swim around the ghostly bridge remains, which was named "Galloping Gertie."

"If you look to the left, May, you can see Fox Island jutting out into the sound. Your property is on this side and has tremendous views of the bridge, sound, and Mount Rainier."

"What were Harvey and Stephanie going to do with that property?"

"It was for investment. He bought the Fox Island land years ago before there was a bridge to the island. In those days there was a small ferry that took islanders back and forth."

"I don't recall going out there with Harvey."

"He didn't go out very much. There was never an intention to build on it. Harvey wanted to be near a golf course so that's how he came to build in Gig Harbor. He was correct in his assumption that land values would go up on Fox Island."

We turned onto the second Gig Harbor exit and followed the street down a steep hill that overlooked the picturesque little town and inlet. Fishing and pleasure boats were moored along the water. Restaurants, gift shops, and other tourist-oriented businesses help the town stay alive. Fishing had once been the primary source of income, but those days were gone. Now tourists clogged the streets and sidewalks. We turned right near the bottom of the hill and pulled in front of the bank.

"We're here. Let me give you the key before we go in," Albert said. He pulled a key from his wallet and handed it to me.

We got out of the car and walked toward the bank. It was a small branch and didn't look much larger than my little house in the North End.

"Why didn't Harvey use the main branch in Tacoma?"

"He lived here and liked the small town atmosphere. He rarely came into Tacoma anymore. He was almost to the point of being fully retired, just a matter of getting paperwork through the system."

"It is pretty out here, isn't it?" The quaint harbor town reminded me of pictures by Currier and Ives. "I can understand why he and Stephanie wanted to live here."

We walked into the lobby and went to the counter. "Can I help you?" A young woman asked. She wasn't wearing a nametag.

"I need to open a safety deposit box."

"Here's her paperwork," Albert said, as he placed what looked to me like a library card on the counter.

"Right this way, Miss Scott," she said reading my name from the card.

"I'll be sitting right over there, May. Take all the time you need," Albert said, as he headed for a comfortable looking chair.

I followed her back to a door that she unlocked and into a small, windowless room. I knew I wouldn't be able to stay long because it was making me claustrophobic before I'd set a foot inside. Things that never used to bother me were beginning to take over my life. I began seeing black spots before my eyes and I leaned over, grabbed my knees, and took some deep breaths.

"Are you all right?" she asked in alarm.

"Yes, just let me try to rise up. I can't be in confined places without windows," I said, trying to regain control. I didn't tell her it had started a few days ago when someone had tried to murder me. After a few seconds I walked into the room and stood by a counter that was along the wall.

"Would you like me to get the box for you?"

"Please."

"I'll need your key," she said.

She went over to a floor to ceiling wall of various sized boxes. Using the keys, she opened one of the smaller ones and pulled out what looked like a steel shoebox. She brought it to the counter where I was leaning and placed it in front of me.

"Would you like me to open the lid?" she asked.

"I can do it. Thank you for your help."

140

"Should I leave you alone now, will you be all right?"

"I think so. If you could just wait by the door, please."

"Certainly."

She walked over and stood with her back to me. I would have to write her a thank you note when this was over. I was sure this was the strangest day she'd had in a while.

I slowly opened the lid and looked inside. There was a large manila envelope stuffed tightly in the box. I pulled it out, checked to see if anything else was in the bottom and closed the lid. I knew I couldn't open it now. I'd do that when I was alone in my comfortable North End house.

I walked to the door and the young woman turned around. "I don't know your name but you've been very helpful. Thank you," I said.

"My name is Rhonda and you're welcome."

I found Albert reading a sports magazine. He looked up as I walked over to him. "That didn't take long."

"No, it didn't."

He didn't ask but I knew he was curious as to the contents of the heavy envelope I held. All I wanted to do was to go back to my safe little house and take a nap. I was exhausted and wanted to be alone. After I'd rested, I'd open the envelope.

"If you don't mind," I asked. "Could we look at the Gig Harbor house and the Fox Island property on another visit? I'm really tired."

"Absolutely. I'll have you back to Tacoma in no time flat."

I thought he was kidding but he was correct. Traffic wasn't heavy going to Tacoma this time of the afternoon. Of course, during the morning commute, it would be a nightmare.

# Twenty-three

In fifteen minutes we were in front of the law offices. "Would you like to come in, May?" Albert asked politely.

"I'd like to go home now. Is there anything else I need to do?"

"We've covered the will thoroughly, you opened the deposit box, and have the contents in your possession. Would you like to join my wife and me for dinner tonight at our condo? I could go over any questions that you might have, after you've had time to rest."

"Thank you for the offer but I planned on having dinner with an old friend of mine. I don't get to see her often so I'm looking forward to it. Maybe on my next visit I can join you and your wife for dinner. Will Ronnie be taking me to the airport in the morning? I should be on the road by seven. Also, I'll have to stop by the police station and return the vest and gun I borrowed."

"He'll be at your place by six-thirty. When does your flight leave?"

"Nine and I'll arrive in Las Vegas at eleven. I told my partner I'd meet him at the office by noon. It'll be tight, but I should make it."

"I guess this will be goodbye, then.

"You and Ronnie have made this trip, which I've been dreading, pleasant under the circumstances. We'll be in touch, I'm sure."

"Absolutely. Anything at all I can do let me know. I'll drive you to your car. Where did you park?"

"It's around the corner. By the way, I guess I'm going to need a new attorney. Would you be interested in taking me on?"

"My pleasure. Harvey was right about you. He said you were a rough cut gem."

I smiled. That was the nicest description of me I'd ever heard. What I wanted now was to uncover the gem part.

I drove back to my house and felt relief when I watched the garage door close. I was back in my little cocoon. I walked into the kitchen, plopped my purse and the large envelope on top of the counter, just as my cell phone rang.

"May, sorry I haven't called but it's been wild today," Ed said.

"I've left a few messages for you, but I knew you were busy. What's the news with Rick's murder? Stun gun, clean shot to the head like the others?"

"Exactly. We've trying to locate Dickie Patty."

"Dickie Patty? Do you think he's the killer?"

"Brenda's been working that angle hard and we know he's been defrauding the development company. Of course, they only knew him as Diana."

"But did he kill all of those people, Ed?"

"Right now we can't prove anything, other than the fraud. He's a person of interest, though. He did have contact with you, Harvey and Stephanie – all of you visited the housing area. Papers related to the will were taken from Rick's office. If he was looking for something that he thought would incriminate him that would explain your house getting ripped apart, and the attacks on you. Maybe he thought one of you had caught onto his scam. Let's face it; you and Harvey are cops. Dickie knew that and cops would make him very nervous. He had close to a million dollars pilfered away in an account in the Cayman Islands. I'd say that would be enough of a motive for murder. He's a physical match, too, based on that tape we got from the hospital when Lomas was killed. We've been checking out Harvey and Stephanie's relatives, thinking they might be upset about the will. So far that's gotten us nowhere."

"Sounds like Dickie might be a suspect but the rest are dead-ends?"

"That sums it up, I'm afraid. You know, though, the connecting piece in all of the murders is you. How's it going? Did you get the vest and gun?"

"Sure did. Have it on right now, as a matter of fact. Do you have any leads on Dickie's whereabouts?"

"Right now, no. But every cop in the southwest knows about him. What was in the safety deposit box?"

"I haven't opened it yet."

"I thought that was the purpose of your trip to Tacoma."

"I did open the box. I just haven't opened the envelope that was in it."

"Why not? That makes no sense, May."

"It does to me. I'll let you know first what's in the envelope."

"I figured it would be rubies and diamonds, as crazy as that old guy was about you."

"I don't like the sound of that statement."

"Yeah, I guess that was sort of mean, wasn't it?"

"To say the least."

"Are you still planning on getting back here tomorrow at noon?"

"Yes, I should be in the office right about then. My plane lands at eleven."

"Are you going anywhere else this afternoon or tonight?" His voice sounded anxious.

"I hope to have dinner with a girlfriend, if she's not busy. I haven't called her yet, so it'll be last minute."

"That sounds like the May I know. I wish you'd stay in and not go prowling all over Tacoma."

"You sound like Janet mother-henning me."

"We're concerned about your safety."

"I know that. I'll be careful."

I hung up and put my phone back into my purse. I looked at the envelope and thought about opening it. I wasn't sure if I wanted to know what was in it. Maybe it would be another gift, as Ed mentioned. I hoped not. Although, what Albert said to me earlier was true; I could use what Harvey had left me to help others. I lifted the heavy envelope, turned it over and put it down. I'd open it later. Right now I was hungry.

After I heated soup and ate it with a sandwich I felt better. I called Betty and left a message, both at work and home. She'd be mad that I hadn't called earlier, but there was nothing I could do about that. Until I heard from her, I'd take a nap. I lay down on top of the covers and rolled up in them. I fell asleep in less than five minutes.

The ringing doorbell woke me up. For a moment, I wasn't sure where I was. I'd slept in so many different beds lately I was confused. I unrolled from the covers, got up and padded to the front door. I saw Betty's mop of uncontrolled salt-and-pepper hair and granny-glasses through the little peephole.

I unlocked the door, pulled it open, and smiled up at my tall, pudgy friend. "You are a sight for sore eyes, girlie." Betty was younger than me, but she looked older. She dressed in a way that made her figure look even bulkier than it was. She looked like what she was – a slightly eccentric rumpled professor.

"Don't call me girlie. You look terrible. You've lost weight. Why haven't you called me? Can I come in or should I just stand out here on the porch?"

"Which question do you want me to answer first? But do come in," I grinned as I took her in my arms. "I've missed you."

"Me, too. When are you going to move back to Tacoma and get away from that horrible Las Vegas and that ghastly hot weather?"

"I see you haven't lost any of your charm."

"Well, it's the truth. You must be out of your mind to live in a place like that."

"Come on, now, tell me what you really think. Don't hold back," I teased.

"What's happened to this house? It looks good. It never looked like this before. I thought you sold it. What's going on?"

"Come in, get comfortable, and I'll tell you a story you aren't going to believe," I said as I maneuvered her to the couch. "Do you want tea, coffee or something stronger?"

"Do you have any wine?"

"I don't know. Let me check."

I wasn't surprised to find bottles of merlot and zinfandel in the pantry. "This hasn't been chilled, do you still want it?" I asked, completely baffled by what to do with the wine.

Betty walked over to the counter, selected the merlot and proceeded to rummage through drawers for an opener. "Where is it?" she asked.

"I don't know. Keep looking, you'll find it."

I decided to make myself a few cups of coffee. Betty opened the bottle and poured a glass of the burgundy colored wine into a pretty stemmed glass she found in the cupboard.

"Okay, let's hear it," she said, as she sipped the wine.

"Let me start at the beginning."

By the time I'd finished, she'd consumed most of the wine and I'd gone through two pots of coffee. Betty looked at me over her small-framed, thick glasses and said, "That story is so nuts I'd think anybody else telling me such stuff would be lying. With you, it's par for the course. Your life has never been dull."

I've always admired the way Betty could cut right to the heart of an issue. She believed in scalpel clean rapid dissections, not of bodies but emotions. She's one of the few non-touchy-feely psychologists I've met.

"You miss having me around to pick on, don't you?" I grinned.

"You have provided me with years of entertainment. And I don't have to pay a cable fee to get it, either," she responded.

"This is nothing more than entertainment, huh?"

"No, it's serious. Scary serious. But it's easier to make light of it, don't you think?"

"Well, with you it is. Of course, as I listened to myself describe the last several days it does sound unbelievable and I lived it."

"Do you have on your vest?"

"Yes."

"Is it uncomfortable?"

"Yes, and heavy. I put the inserts in, so it's the real deal."

"What does 'real deal' mean?"

"I'm like superman – bullets won't get through."

"I thought all vests were bullet-proof."

"Nope. Vests would stop shrapnel, but not a bullet. With the insert, bullets shouldn't penetrate my chest."

"What if you're not hit in the chest? You told me the killer has been shooting people in the head."

I looked at my dear friend and didn't say anything.

Her eyes widened and filled with tears. "Oh, now I get it."

"Stop crying! I'm alive and sitting here. I like it better when you're picking on me."

"Why do you stay in police work? It's so demeaning and cruel, and it seems the good guys are the ones who die."

"You know better than that, Betty. If you don't watch it, I'm going to spread the truth about you all over Tacoma – you're a marshmallow inside."

"I am when it comes to friends I've had for years."

Betty and I had met at the University of Puget Sound. She'd been one of my instructors – the only one who wouldn't accept any of my lame excuses for why I hadn't done a paper or arrived on time for class. She was relentless in trying to get me to reform and follow the rules, especially those she'd created. From animosity, our friendship grew.

"Let's change the subject. Are you hungry? Do you want to go to dinner?" I asked.

"I'm too drunk to go anywhere. Let's just eat something from this well-stocked kitchen of yours."

We scurried around and within an hour we'd prepared a delicious-smelling pasta dinner. I set the small round table that looked out onto my beautiful backyard. "Maybe I should consider moving back here," I said, although I knew I'd never do it.

"That's the smartest thing I've heard you say since I walked in the door. Can you believe it's almost eight? What time is your plane leaving in the morning?"

"Nine."

"When are you coming back?"

"When all this has ended, I guess. I've asked Albert to be my lawyer so my Tacoma connection will always exist."

"Have you given any thought to what you'll do with all the money and property?"

"Not much. I suspect I'll take early retirement and build a house somewhere on the fifty acres I own in Pahrump."

"Isn't it isolated out there? I can't understand your attraction for that barren desert."

"It does take time to develop an appreciation for high desert country. For me it came easier because it reminds me of Montana. I like the wide-open spaces; the way the sky is so huge and blue. And, of course, I do love that warm Nevada sunshine."

We made quick work of the pasta and Betty joined me in a cup of coffee.

"Do you think this David person will finally be the guy for you?"

"Who knows? You know my track record there. It's not pretty."

"You never have had any sense about men, that's for sure. You should do what I do and just ignore the whole lot of them."

"Yeah, you've always been 'little-miss-goody-two-shoes-celibate-nun-type'."

"You don't get hurt that way."

"Yes, you do. It's got to be lonely. I mean, I have relationships with men and as much as I've been hurt, I wouldn't change a thing about my past."

"The guy who loved you the most was Harvey."

"I wouldn't quibble with that. But it was a father-daughter thing and that's different than what we're talking about."

"He would have loved you the other way, if you'd let him." Her eyes took on that psychologist glint that I didn't like

"Don't go there. You know how that sets me off. It wasn't true. It was never that way. You, of all people, should know that."

"Just giving my opinion."

"Yeah, and I know how you love to do that, girlie."

"Don't call me 'girlie'. Okay, I have to ask this. Have you called him?"

"Who?" I asked innocently.

"Don't give me that crap. Dan, that's who. He's part of the reason you got on a plane and came up here, isn't he?" She sat her coffee cup down carefully on the small table.

"No!"

"Liar. You still love that good-for-nothing-two-timing-piece-of…"

"I get your drift. You were right every inch of the way. I never should have married him. Let's change the subject."

"Now you believe me. And you still love him, even after all he did to you."

"I do not!"

"You tell me how you like the sunshine and heat in Nevada. The real reason you're there, in that horrible desert, is because you ran away when Dan left you for Connie. Then they went and had twins. It ripped you apart and you went howling off to Las Vegas like a scalded dog."

I loved Betty, but she could also drive me crazy. "Time to stop. Don't want to hear any of this."

"That means you need to hear it."

"I have an idea. Go drink another bottle of wine. Then you'll be too drunk to pick on me."

"I'm not picking on you. I asked you a simple question. Are you going to call Dan?"

"No. Now, change the subject, *girlie.*"

We spent another couple of hours talking. It was enjoyable, after she let up about Dan. Betty and I might be polar opposites, but somehow we harmonized. When she got ready to leave, both of us were teary-eyed.

"Look at me, I'm a crying mess. And I'm still half-drunk."

"Do you want to spend the night here?" I asked.

"No, I have to be up early. I have several students coming in to see me early tomorrow plus two classes to teach in the morning. I want you to call me and keep me up to date on your situation. When you get that house built in Pahrump I'll come visit."

"You'll be my first house guest."

"Listen, I know we joked around, but you be careful. Keep that vest on even if it doesn't do that much good."

I promised her I would. I stood on the porch and waved until her car lights disappeared into the night.

# Twenty-four

It didn't take long to get the house back in order and pack. I set the coffee pot to brew at six so I wouldn't have to mess with it in the morning. When Betty and I were making dinner I'd moved the envelope from the kitchen into the bedroom. As I picked up the few items I'd brought and put them into my small suitcase, I shook the envelope. It was tightly packed and nothing rattled. Ed was wrong – there weren't rubies and diamonds inside. I placed it in the top of my zippered carry-on bag, which was my only luggage. My goal was to open it on the plane. That way I'd have two uninterrupted hours to look at whatever it was Harvey had left for me.

I walked around and looked at the lovely house. I didn't want to leave it. Maybe I'd take Harvey up on the offer he'd never got to present to me – spend half the year in Nevada and the other half in Tacoma. Unless I wanted to, I didn't have to work anymore. I could buy anything, go anywhere and lack of finances wouldn't stop me.

My life had centered on work and the people involved with law enforcement. It was hard to comprehend that way of life was about to change. Now I could understand why some people are reluctant to retire. When they finally do, they often return to work within a few months. I used to feel sorry for them because they couldn't figure out what to do with the hours they had to fill. Now I understood – it's scary having all those unknown options in front of you. Albert said I was lucky. Maybe so; but at this moment, I felt lonely and afraid.

Ronnie was punctual. I'd been up since five, nervous to get going,

151

yet not wanting to leave. When I saw his shiny, black truck pull in the driveway I gathered up my purse, suitcase, and went out to meet him. I locked the door to the kitchen, laundry room, and pushed the button to raise the garage door. After I'd stepped outside the garage, I pushed another button that was alongside the door to close it. I took a quick look around, wished I could stay longer, and then got in the truck with Ronnie.

"Thanks for getting up so early. And here are the keys to the house and car," I said, as I laid the keys in one of the cup holders.

"No problem. Uncle Albert said you needed to stop by the Tacoma Police Department?"

"I have a gun and vest to return. I borrowed them during my stay."

"No problem. We'll be there in five minutes."

It took a little longer than five minutes, but not much. That was one thing I'd liked about where I lived in Tacoma – it was close to work and I didn't have to deal with clogged freeways.

Ronnie parked in front of the building. I got out and had no trouble getting past security. I walked back to Property Control. Sergeant Nelson wasn't it, but that didn't make it harder. The young woman on duty must have known I was coming. She had the paperwork ready for me. I turned in the two items, signed some papers, she gave me a copy, and I was back in the truck within minutes.

"That didn't take long," Ronnie said, as I strapped myself into the seatbelt.

"This whole trip has been easy," I replied. I buckled myself into the seatbelt.

We didn't talk too much on the way to SeaTac Airport. The freeway was very crowded. For part of the trip, it was stop and go, especially when we got to Federal Way and Auburn. A drive that had taken fifteen minutes a couple of nights ago took forty-five minutes this morning.

"You're lucky, May. I was afraid it'd be a lot worse out here. We're practically flying up I-5," Ronnie said, as we crawled our way along the freeway. It made me long for the empty stretches of desert highway around Pahrump.

The check-in process with multiple bag inspections took longer than I'd anticipated. SeaTac did things slower than the Las Vegas terminal. By the time I'd finished the gauntlet, my flight was boarding. When I made it to my seat and put my bag in front of my feet, I was ready for a nap. Luckily no one sat next to me so I didn't have to chat. I wasn't in a mood to be friendly. All I wanted to do was curl under the airline blanket and sleep, which is what I did.

I woke up when I felt the wheels touch down. I leaned over and saw the caramel-colored mountains that surround Las Vegas. I sighed with relief. It felt good to be home.

It didn't take long to make my way through the terminal and to my car. I drove to the exit, paid, and headed for the office. I'd forgotten to bring my sunglasses and I needed them. Being in the Northwest for a few days had made my eyes more sensitive to the bright, desert sunshine. The warm weather penetrated into my bones and I felt myself unwind. I hit the button to lower the driver side window and sucked in the dry desert air.

I pulled into the parking lot at two minutes before noon, raced through the doors and made it to my desk, announcing, "I'm right on time."

Ed and Brenda smiled and I knew they were pleased to have me back. That felt good; I was glad to be part of the team again.

"How was your trip?" Brenda asked.

"It went amazingly well. I hired Albert Catrel as my attorney. Is there any news about Dickie Patty?"

"Not so far," Ed answered. "What was in the envelope?"

I was beginning to feel foolish about the answer "I haven't opened it yet."

Both Ed and Brenda turned their tall, lithe bodies in my direction. I saw the same mystified look from each of them.

"Ed, Brenda, get in here!" Lieutenant Frank called from his office. "Oh, hello, May. You're not supposed to be back at work yet. We'll call you when something happens," he said curtly.

"Sorry, May. The boss is calling," Brenda said, as she lightly touched me on the shoulder. "I'll call you later this afternoon. Maybe we could have dinner tonight?"

"Maybe so," I said, with a sinking feeling. I wasn't part of the team after all.

# Twenty-five

I called David from the phone on Brenda's desk. I couldn't use my desk because it had been taken over by a person I didn't recognize. I'd only been away for a few days and I felt like an outsider.

David didn't answer his office phone so I left a message telling him I was on the way out to his house. His schedule was so busy that we hadn't seen that much of each other before I'd left on the trip to Tacoma. That suited me fine. I wasn't ready for a relationship of any sort with a man. I felt like my skin was raw from war wounds and I needed a quiet place to heal. The lieutenant was right – I shouldn't be at work.

I picked up my purse and made my way out to the car, putting on my sunglasses as I pushed opened the large, glass door. Tacoma had been sunny but cool, nothing like the intensity of Nevada heat. Before I got behind the wheel, I stood for a moment and soaked up the warmth because it felt so good. I really did hate being cold. As much as I enjoyed Tacoma, it wasn't warm enough for me to want to live there on a permanent basis.

I reached David's house in less than fifteen minutes. I got out of the car, opened the trunk and got my suitcase. I closed the lid and clumsily walked toward the front door, trying to keep the suitcase out of the dust. David should do something to the front yard so it wasn't such a dust bowl. I liked natural landscaping, but this was going too far. Every step I took created a dusty little whirlpool around my legs. When I reached the steps, I pushed the suitcase onto the small deck. I searched through my purse for a tissue so I could wipe away the fine layer of dust that covered my black shoes. I didn't want to track it onto his carpeted floors. For a man, he kept a clean house. Some of that was due to the fact he was gone so much and no one was around to mess it up.

I picked up the fake geranium plant and searched for the house key David kept stuck down the side of the pot. I pulled it out, put the plant back where it had been, and opened the door. I heard the grandmother clock ticking inside the house. It sounded lonesome. As I picked up my suitcase, I took a quick backward glance at the yard and the dirt road leading to his house. No one was there that I could see. Still, it made me feel eerie.

I quickly pulled the door shut behind me and locked it. As soon as I did that I realized I hadn't put the house key back in the pot. I re-opened the door, peeped outside, and stepped onto the deck. I reached for the pot, the phone rang and I jumped. I was so nervous I almost dropped the plant. I shoved the key down the side of the plant, backed into the house and locked the door again. The phone rang incessantly and I let it. I figured the message would be for David, not me. He'd programmed the phone so I heard the message as it recorded.

"This is Molly from the Medical Examiner's Office. May, please come to the morgue as soon as you can. Dr. Williams needs to see you right away."

I was surprised to hear that and I tried to answer but Molly had hung up by the time I picked up the receiver. How did they know that I was here? No one knew except those working the case. Of course, that did include Dr. Williams and Molly. I had to get my paranoia under control.

I stood in David's quiet, neat house and tried to figure out when I'd started to get so scared. Where had that come from all of a sudden? I walked into the kitchen and opened the refrigerator. He always kept orange juice, so I took the carton out and poured myself a glass. As I drank it I walked around aimlessly. When I passed his bedroom I glanced in and my eyes settled on a piece of paper that was on top of his bed pillow. Everything else looked so neat and orderly that it seemed out of place.

I went into his room, sat the glass down on the dresser and picked up the sheet of paper. One sentence, written in red, was scrawled on it in a haphazard pattern:

"May will die."

I dropped the paper like it had burned my fingers. Had David written that sentence? Had I walked willingly into the killer's lair?

My pulse pounded and my breath was rapid and shallow. Black spots were in front of my eyes and I leaned over and grasped my knees to try and stop myself from passing out. I fell to my knees and lowered my head to the floor. Was David the killer? He certainly fit the profile, tall and slender. I thought back and that didn't make sense, but nothing did anymore. I'd lost all objectivity and was caught in an emotional storm. I stayed in that position for a couple of minutes, until I felt strong enough to stand. I realized I'd have to give the piece of paper to Ed and Brenda. I could do that after I'd talked with Dr. Williams.

Quickly, I went through the house and gathered my few belongings, especially my gun, which I'd hidden in the back of the linen closet, under the sheets. Maybe I'd had a premonition about this before I opened the front door. Perhaps that's why I'd been so nervous. I felt the killer's presence around me. He was closing in and it terrified me.

I got my suitcase back into the trunk of the car, opened the passenger door and put my purse, with my gun inside, on the seat. I'd put the three-word message from the killer into a paper bag, which I placed carefully onto the floor of the front seat. I knew forensics would go over it for any traces of fingerprints, the type of ink and paper that was used, and the style of writing. I walked back onto the deck, closed and locked the front door. I looked around and it seemed peaceful and quiet. I heard a plane overheard, heading for McCarran, or maybe it was an Air Force jet on its way to Nellis. That reminded me that I needed to call Janet and ask how things were going. I guessed she and Frankie still lived on base, where they'd be safe.

I got into the car, locked the doors, and turned the ignition so the air conditioner would come on. I pulled out my phone and called Ed.

He wasn't answering so I left a message about the note and that I was on my way to the morgue, as Dr. Williams had requested. Next, I called Janet and left her the same message and asked about Whiskers. I promised Janet I'd find a hotel to stay in that would let me keep Whiskers in the room.

Traffic had thickened and it took longer than normal to get to the morgue. I pulled into the lot and the first vacant parking space I could find and locked the car.

Before I walked into the building I took a few moments to soak up the warmth of the sunshine once again. The sky was cloudless and the breeze felt soft as it brushed over my skin. If it wasn't for the traffic noise, I'm sure I could have heard birds chirping. Landscape crews were putting in palm trees, shrubbery and grass around the new building. By the time they finished, it would resemble the rest of the area, which was aptly named "Oasis."

I opened the large, glass door and walked to the last unmarked elevator that led to the morgue. I punched in the code and the doors whisked open. It only took a few moments before they opened again and I walked down the long hall toward yet another set of unmarked doors. I punched in another code on the keypad, pushed my way into the office area and called out for Dr. Williams and Molly. I stood for a moment and didn't hear any reply so I walked back toward the "body room" as Ed sometimes called it.

"Dr. Williams, Molly?" I called again, looking around at the large room. "I'm here, just like you asked me to be."

Two sheet-covered bodies were on the stainless steel gurneys, probably new arrivals awaiting their autopsies. Along the back wall, autopsied bodies were stored in individual refrigerated coolers until they were ready for their next destination, usually a funeral home. I wondered if Harvey and Stephanie were still here. The time-released, ceiling-mounted deodorizers clicked on and the smell was pungent. I could never work full-time in this place. For one thing, I was getting cold.

"Dr. Williams, Molly?" If they didn't show up in the next second, I was out of here.

I heard a sound behind me. I didn't want to look but I knew I had to. When I did, I wished I hadn't.

A body, covered in a white sheet, rose to a sitting position on the gurney behind me. Then a hand reached out and pulled the covering away to reveal a tall, slender body. A black hood, with eye, nose, and mouth openings covered his head. His torso and legs were encased in what appeared to be a black wetsuit, like divers wear. Black boots, military-style, covered his small feet. He swung his legs over the table and stood, towering over my small frame, not saying a word.

I took a step backwards and stumbled into the gurney with the other sheet-covered body on it. I grabbed the sheet off the body and threw it at the killer, hoping to give myself a few seconds to run. I turned and ran toward the doors, fumbling in my purse for my gun. I pulled it out, intent on using it, when I felt the peculiar sensation of electric currents stunning my back. I hadn't worn my vest. It was in my car trunk. That was the last thought I remembered before waking up again.

\* \* \* \*

I woke up colder than I've ever been in my life. I reached down to find the covers to pull up around me. I wondered if Whiskers was on the bed with me. Usually she sleeps near my feet and keeps them warm. When I tried to rise up I bumped my head. I opened my eyes and realized I wasn't in my bedroom. I couldn't tell where I was because it was so dark. I felt around and found that I was enclosed in some sort of small area, just the right size for a body, with no excess room. There was a covering on me and it felt like a heavy, cotton sheet. I reached underneath my body and felt the cold, steel table. I knew where I was, but my mind couldn't process the horror of the thought.

I searched around with my hands, hoping that the killer had put my purse next to me; he hadn't. If I had my gun, I'd shoot my way out of here, right after I'd used my cell phone to call Ed. I reached up and back, trying to determine which way I'd been placed in the cooler.

159

The wall felt smooth so I guessed my feet must be at the door. I slid down the table and using my feet, tried to pound the steel door open. I kept it up until my legs started cramping from the cold. I waited a few seconds for the worst of the cramps to leave my legs and then I started pounding the door again, screaming, "Help! Get me out of here!"

I kept up the pounding and screaming for what seemed like hours, but it couldn't have been. The coolers were kept at forty degrees and oxygen would last, possibly, for thirty minutes to an hour. If lack of oxygen didn't kill me, hypothermia would. Between times I tried to listen for outside noises, but the cooler was solid and I couldn't hear anything. I kept up the pounding and screaming, knowing that if someone didn't come soon, the killer would have his wish, and I would be dead.

When the cooler door opened and the table was pulled out I didn't know if I was dreaming or not. I tried to raise my hand to shield my eyes from the bright light but I couldn't lift my arm. I felt hands lifting me onto a stretcher and a blanket was placed over me. Ed leaned down and talked to me; his words didn't make sense, though. I tried to respond but my mouth wouldn't move. Dr. Williams hovered over me and I tried to push his hands away. I was afraid I was already dead and he was going to start my autopsy.

# Twenty-Six

"May, can you hear me? Talk to me, hon. Say something, please!"

Through a swirling fog I heard Janet's voice call me back from where ever I'd been. My eyes wouldn't open easily; they were stuck together with gritty goop that felt like bits of gravel when I tried to rub it away.

"Am I dead?"

"No, you survived, again. You're in the hospital. The same room you've been in twice before in the past couple of weeks."

"How's Whiskers? I promise I'll take her away, Janet, just as soon as I get out of here."

Now that my sight was restored and the fog had lifted, her beautiful face smiled down at me. She looked like an angel.

"Are you sure I'm not dead?"

"No, but it's not because the murderer isn't trying to kill you. He almost did it this time."

"Was I in the cooler a long time?"

"Long enough. It's a good thing you made those calls to Ed and me about going to the morgue."

"I wanted you to know because I think David might be the killer. I'd thought it was Dickie Patty, but I don't know. I'm not sure of anything anymore, Janet."

"I know. You've been through hell and back. For a small woman, you've got a lot of fight in you. You should see the doors to the cooler where you kicked them. Very impressive."

"Is Ed here?"

"He's still at the morgue. In fact, when you called, we were at another crime scene. That's how we knew you were in serious trouble, because Doc Williams was with us. And he knew nothing about Molly calling you. She's on vacation this week."

"I was saved by the messages I left for you and Ed'."

"Yes, you were. Does your back hurt where the stun gun hit you?"

"It's sore. How long have I been here?"

Janet looked at her watch. "Two hours."

I sat up, turned back the covers, and swung my legs over the edge of the hospital bed. I unhooked myself from the one tube that held me hostage and slid my feet onto the cold, tile floor.

"What do you think you're doing?"

"I'm leaving. I don't like hospitals, I'm not sick, so I'm out of here."

"No, you're not going anywhere. There's an officer outside your door. You're under house arrest, sort of."

"Nope, not again. I need to leave."

I heard a phone ring in a drawer next to the bed. I opened the drawer, found my purse, and pulled out my phone.

"Hello."

The disguised voice I'd heard before said, "Let's meet one last time, May, at Red Rock Canyon. You know where I'll be. Come alone." The connection went dead.

"Who was that? You've turned white as a sheet."

"He wants me to meet him. Where we had a bottle of wine together."

"Whom're you talking about?"

"David."

"The guy you've been staying with? The helicopter pilot who's in the Air Force Reserve?"

"Yes."

"You're wrong, May, he's not the killer."

"Did you see the piece of paper I found at his house? And the killer is tall and thin, just like David. Now he wants me to meet him where we had our first date, if that's what it's called these days."

"In that case, Dickie Patty is tall, thin and lives next to Red Rock Canyon. He does live in Blue Diamond, doesn't he?"

"Yes," I admitted, seeing the inconsistencies Janet had pointed out. "You don't think either one of them is the killer? Then tell me who is?"

"I don't know and neither do you. I do know that you need to get back in that bed. You were about dead this time, my friend. So crawl into bed and cover up."

"No, I won't stay here. I'm going out to Red Rock Canyon and get this over with. I'm tired of being afraid and running. I want to get this guy and he wants me, too. That's why he keeps coming after me." As I talked I threw off the hospital gown and got into my clothes. "Where are my car keys?" I asked Janet as I rummaged through my small purse.

"With your car. It's a crime scene and it's impounded."

"How am I supposed to get out to Red Rock?"

"You're not. That's the point."

"Janet, you know I can't just stay here. Let me borrow your car."

"No."

"Please, you know I'm right. I've got to meet this guy head-on and get it over with. He's not going to let up until one of us is dead, Janet, and I promise you, it won't be me."

"You must be out of your mind to think I'm going to let you borrow my car so you can go find this crazy killer alone. What sort of professional police work is that?"

"This isn't about police work. I'm not on this case; remember? This is a score I need to settle for personal reasons."

"I'll drive you out there. Let me go tell the nurses that we're leaving. They told me earlier you wouldn't be staying long. I think they were making bets on how long you'd last before you escaped. I guess you were on this floor last time because they all remember you."

"I left early, that's right. I don't like this place anymore than I like the morgue."

Janet went out the door and I did something I'd never done before.

I went through her purse, got her keys and slipped out the door while she spoke to the nurses. I didn't want her anywhere near the killer. It was going to be him and me.

After I walked down the hall, in the opposite direction from the nurse's station and found an elevator, I realized I didn't know where she'd parked.

I walked off the elevator and into the lobby. Signs led the way to the parking garage, and from there it was anybody's guess where Janet's car was located. By now I was certain she'd found out what I'd done. I would apologize to my friend, but I had to do this. Maybe someday she'd understand and forgive me.

I followed a line of people out the door. Since they were lucky enough to know where their cars were parked, they scattered to the four corners and up and down the escalator for other parking levels.

For a few minutes I wandered aimlessly, hoping to catch a glimpse of Janet's silver Honda. It's amazing how many silver cars looked just like hers. I watched as people swirled through the doors, and from quite a distance, in some cases, unlocked their doors with the key remote. I looked down at Janet's remote and clicked it. I didn't hear anything, so I started moving around, clicking as I went. After I'd walked for what seemed a mile or two, I heard the definite click of a door that had just unlocked. I followed where the sound had come from, and there sat the silver Honda. I opened the passenger door, got in and my phone beeped inside my purse. I pulled it out and said, "Hello," certain it was Janet.

"Are you on your way?" the killer asked.

"Yes, I am. I'm going to arrest you and I'll be in the cheering section when the great state of Nevada pulls the plug on your worthless life. You wait for me, because I'm coming. Do you hear me?"

What I heard was laughter. I guess I'd made his day.

I drove out of the hospital parking garage and made my way to the exit that would lead me to Charleston Boulevard and west to Red Rock Canyon. I felt no fear. All I felt was anger. My limit had been reached and as Ed had often said over the years, it wasn't a pretty sight when that happened. There's a fine line between cop and criminal and now, as far as I was concerned, the criminal part of me had taken over. I had no intention of arresting this worthless excuse of a man. I was going to kill him slowly, painfully, and forever. Unlike the horror movies, this monster was going to stay dead.

Traffic had thickened as people left work to go home. It took longer than usual to drive the almost twenty miles to Red Rock Canyon. As I left the non-stop energy of the city behind, the landscape took on an otherworldly look. The steep rock faces of the rugged red canyon dominated the robin's egg-blue sky. The high jagged peaks glowed as the sun struck their striated sandstone faces, turning them copper-colored. As I got closer, I could see where desert varnish, a black-bronze glaze, covered sections of the rock. At the turn off for the Visitor Center, I rummaged around in my purse for money to pay the small entrance fee.

The drive to the first view pullout took about five minutes. There were four cars and one truck parked in the lot and I didn't recognize any of them. When David and I had come out here a few days before, it had been early evening. We'd watched the sunset as the sky turned glowing colors of peach, mauve, pink, yellow and various shades of bluish-purple.

The wind had picked up and dust devils swirled around on the desert floor. I caught a whiff of cigarette smoke and turned to watch as a group of noisy teenagers walked up the steep path toward their truck. I pulled my sunglasses out of my purse and put them on. For a person who'd lived in the southwest for several years, I still had trouble remembering to wear them.

The two girls and two boys got into a red truck and squealed out of the parking lot. It made me appreciate Frankie as I watched the truck careen down the narrow park highway. I came within an inch of calling the park security patrol and giving them the tag number. The teenagers looked like an accident waiting to happen. *Better safe than sorry*, I thought. If I came upon their wrecked truck later I'd really be upset.

Just as I opened my purse to pull out my phone, it rang.

"Stop wasting my time, May. Those kids will do just fine without you calling the cops on them."

"Where are you?" I asked as I turned in a circle looking for him.

"Come find me. You know where I am."

The phone went dead. I punched in the number for park security and let it ring as I walked toward the path David and I had followed. At the top of the steep path I paused and reported what I knew about the truck and the teenagers to the ranger on duty. He said he'd keep an eye out for them. After I'd hung up it dawned on me that I should have told him, "Oh, by the way, I'm on the way to meet a killer." Police procedural had always been a cumbersome chore for me; and one that I'd managed to ignore as much as I could.

Somewhere between the time Harvey and Stephanie had been murdered and now, I'd come to an important decision. This would be my last official act as an officer of the law. I was going to take early retirement and let other people worry about rulebooks and crime.

By the time I started down the trail, the blue sky had turned a shade darker and the wind had picked up. The scent of rain was in the air. In the distance, I saw burros scrambling around the rocky edges of the escarpment, maybe looking for a cave to shelter them from the weather. Flash floods came out of nowhere and the animals knew about them long before hard driving prickles of rain poured from the sky. The high desert was an uncompromising, beautiful, yet brutal area and it seemed the perfect place to end this string of murders.

The gravel path twisted back on itself as I progressed downward. The wind made strange wailing sounds as I followed the well-worn path that was bordered by barrel cactus, prickly pear, and cholla bushes. My slick bottomed shoes weren't suited for this sort of activity. I looked up and the red rocks towered above me as I went deeper into the narrow canyon. It seemed unbelievable that this had once been the ocean floor, in a past so far removed from this moment, that all that remained were skeletons and shells of aquatic life that now helped to form the rocks surrounding me.

I turned another sharp corner and the trail leveled off and then fingered out into four areas; each led to a different view of the canyon floor. Signs warned of getting too close to the edges of the rock outcrops.

No one was there. I watched and listened but only heard the wind as it continued to moan around the reddish-orange walls. The sky looked threatening and I knew it was possible that water could soon cascade down the trail and fall into the dry streambed far below. For a brief time, a river would roar through the twisting, turning path that nature had etched. I'd seen flash floods twice in my life and had been terrified. My heart rate quickened and my breath became shallow. I was paralyzed with fear; not of the killer, but of nature.

I turned and quickly headed up the trail toward higher ground. I figured if I hurried I could make it back to the parking lot before the rain started.

"Where do you think you're going? Are you that much of a coward that you won't face me?"

I turned and faced the killer. "So, it's you. I should have known by the small feet."

"You should have known by lots of things. Where did you put them?"

"Put what?"

"What I've been looking for since I killed Harvey and Stephanie."

"I don't know what that is."

"I thought it was in your house, and then I thought you'd taken them to your hospital room."

"I still don't know what you're talking about."

"When I found out you were in Harvey's will and that he'd sent you on that mission to Tacoma, I realized that's what he'd done with them."

"You're talking about the large envelope I took out of Harvey's deposit box."

"Of course. You know that."

"I never opened it."

"What kind of stupid cop are you? So you had no idea that I was the killer?"

"No, I didn't. Why did you do it? Why did you kill them?"

"Because I loved him. I didn't want anybody else to have him. And I told him so in all those letters."

"It was love letters in that package?"

"I thought they were beautiful love letters. I was so honest with him – I even told him he was going to die. He said I was stalking him." Her face showed disbelief that he would feel that way.

Anne moved closer to me. I didn't see any sign of a weapon. She had on her black, rubber-like cat suit and it made her hair appear white-blonde. I knew I had to keep her talking and away from me. I kept my hands where she could see them. My small gun was tucked up inside my elasticized jacket sleeve. It was a trick Harvey had taught me long ago in Tacoma.

"It was easy for you to get access to the morgue, wasn't it?"

"I have several things going for me. One is the fact that I'm a medical examiner. The other is that I'm beautiful. Don't you think I'm beautiful, May?"

"Yes, you are. Tall, slender and elegant, as well."

"Thank you. Are you ready to die now?"

"No. I still don't understand about Harvey."

"We had an affair when he and I worked together in Chicago. All he ever talked about was you and how he missed you. Then he met Stephanie and dumped me. I figured he didn't deserve to live anymore, so I waited until the right opportunity came along. I'd planned to kill him for a long time. And, like I told you, he knew he was going to die. Did you have an affair with him, too?"

"No, I never did. Harvey and I were the closest of friends." The sky was getting darker and there was a chill in the air.

"Did you know that property out in Pahrump is yours now?"

"What?" I asked in amazement.

"I was with him when he bought it. We'd visited Las Vegas while we were seeing each other and had taken the exact same drive that you and I did the other day."

I remembered Albert Catrel had told me about the property in Pahrump but I didn't recognize it from the legal description.

"He loved you a lot, didn't he?" she asked, moving closer to me.

"Yes, he did. And I loved him. But it wasn't the sort of relationship you had with him. You were special, too, Anne."

"I know. He just made a mistake and married Stephanie instead of me. But that's all fixed. Are you ready to die now? If you'd like, I can do your autopsy. I helped with Harvey and Stephanie's. Did you know that?" The wind blew harder and she used her hand to brush her long hair away from her eyes.

"No, I didn't know that. Why did you kill Mrs. Bride?" I asked, buying more time.

"She knocked on my door – our hotel rooms were next to each other – and told me she knew what I'd done. She tried to blackmail me."

"How about that 'May Will Die' piece of paper I found at David's house?"

"I broke into his house and left it on his pillow. I thought about killing him, too, but I'm getting bored. You'll be my last, at least for a little while," she said as she reached into her jacket pocket, took out a pair of thin, black gloves and put them on.

Raindrops fell in fat plops on the dusty ground. I didn't want to move quickly and startle Anne, but I knew I had to get off the path. I recalled there was a large boulder behind and a little to the right of me.

"I cried a little over Harvey when I was helping with his autopsy, but no one noticed. Did you like being in the cooler?"

"No, that wasn't fun at all. It was really cold," I said as I moved off the path, closer to the boulder.

"It's too bad you have to die. I like you. I believe what you said about your relationship with Harvey. I didn't like killing Stephanie, either."

I took another step and felt the boulder against my back. It was taller than me, so it might provide some protection. "Is that why you put that tarp on top of her body?"

"Yes."

I saw her mouth form the word, but I didn't hear it. There was a deafening roar and a wall of water poured from the sky in a torrent.

I crouched in front of the boulder and made myself as small as I could. I dug my hands and feet into the ground and prayed that the boulder wouldn't be dislodged and tumble into the canyon. The wind and rain slashed at everything in its path. I couldn't see what had happened to Anne because there was a curtain of water in front of me. I leaned my head forward so I could breath; it was like being under deep water, there was so much of it so fast. The only thing that existed in my world was the boulder, the dirt my nails and feet were dug into, and the fury of nature as she battered everything in her path.

I thought I heard a scream, but it might have been the keening of the wind. I felt a slight movement and for a terrified instant, thought the boulder was going to crush me on its way to a watery grave in the newly created river in the canyon below.

It seemed like hours but it was only minutes and I heard another distinctive sound. The rain had slowed and the swooshing sound of a helicopter was overhead. I knew it was David's as soon as I looked up and saw it. He flew it down as low as he could and waved, as did Ed, who was sitting next to him.

I sat still for a few moments as the rain and wind slackened and stopped. Carefully I crawled and slid my way down to the outcrop and looked over the edge. The raging river was already starting to subside. Anne's body was sprawled on the rocks about halfway down the cliff. It was evident she was dead. I slowly worked my way up toward the parking lot. I watched as the helicopter circled and landed, knowing that I was safe.

# Epilogue

"Stop it, Aunt May, you're embarrassing me," Frankie said, as I took another photo with my new digital camera.

"Let me get one more of you, Kim, and your folks." They stood in front of Janet's rose bushes, which bordered her front steps. She and Frankie had moved back home and Tom had joined them.

"Don't you think you should comb your hair again?" grinned David, as he pretended to pat down Frankie's military-style buzz cut.

"Look how wonderful they look," I responded as I clicked away.

"And we're not going anywhere," Tom and Janet said in unison.

"You two are made for each other," I grinned, as they looked lovingly at each other and leaned in for a quick kiss.

"It's time for Kim and me to go. The limo driver is going to leave without us. We'll miss our dinner reservations at the Stratosphere."

"I know. I'm being silly. It's so great to see all of you together and looking so happy. Kim, you are one lucky girl to be included in this family."

Kim's dark, almond-shaped eyes sparkled and her shoulder-length, shiny black hair swung as she agreed, "It's like a dream. I've had a crush on Frankie for three years, ever since I was a freshman."

Frankie blushed, we laughed, and I continued to snap pictures.

I heard my cell phone ringing in my purse and I handed the camera to David.

"Take pictures of them in the limo while I get this call."

I pulled my small phone out of my purse and opened it. "Hello."

"Don't hang up, May. Just listen to me. I've been thinking about you a lot lately. I'm coming down to Las Vegas for a meeting and thought we could get together. I've missed you, babe," my ex-husband said in the breathless manner that I used to think was so sexy.

"Stay away from me!" I hissed, hoping no one noticed that I'd turned my back and walked away from my friends.

"You miss me, too, don't you, baby? We were so good together."

I stared at the phone in disbelief. Then I turned it off and stuffed it back in my purse.

"Who was that?" David asked, as he came up behind me. "You look like you've been talking to a ghost."

I turned and smiled at him. "It was a wrong number."

I reached for his hand and we walked back toward the house.